THE CARETAKER

EMILY SHINER

INKUBATOR
BOOKS

Published by Inkubator Books
www.inkubatorbooks.com

Copyright © 2022 by Emily Shiner

Emily Shiner has asserted her right to be identified as the author of this work.

ISBN (eBook): 978-1-915275-37-0
ISBN (Paperback): 978-1-915275-38-7
ISBN (Hardback): 978-1-915275-39-4

PROLOGUE
PAUL

I promised my wife I wouldn't ever forget her after she died.

I promised the same thing to my daughter, telling Holly over and over that things would get better. I held her while she sobbed into my chest, running my fingers through her hair and down her back. Her mother should have been here to comfort her now. Wilma was always better at it than me.

She'd always known what to say and how to handle the situation when someone was upset. I shut down and left her to deal with everything emotional.

Only now she can't.

"It's going to be fine," I tell Holly, finally pulling back from her. Holly looks up at me with red-rimmed eyes and puffy cheeks.

I want to tug at my shirt, pull it away from my body. She's cried into the fabric so much that it's stuck to me, but the look on her face keeps me from moving.

Before she speaks, she drags her arm across her cheeks to

wipe away her tears. "You have to fix this," she tells me, and there's anger in her voice.

A weak current runs through her and into me when I reach out and touch her shoulder. I'm so tired of worrying, tired of being exhausted, and this jolt of anger is like a shot of caffeine straight to my system.

"I can't fix this," I tell her. "Your mom is gone. As much as I'd like to, there's no way to bring her back and—"

"I didn't ask you to bring her back. I said you need to fix this, Dad." She's breathing harder, her eyes locked on mine.

"I can't fix this."

"You can. You can hurt them. They hurt her, and they don't deserve to be happy. Why would you be okay with someone being happy after what they did to Mom?"

I wipe sweat off my forehead before finally plucking my shirt away from my body. It's hot in here, the air thick and heavy. Even the ceiling fan that I installed last year to try to swirl away the heat from the late days of summer isn't doing its job. It's moving in slow circles like putting more effort into spinning would be too much work.

"You know revenge won't solve anything." I want to get through to her and make sure she understands that acting impulsively right now is a terrible idea. I want her mom back as much as she does, but we can't do anything rash. "If you do something and get caught, then I'll lose you, and I can't let that happen. Not after I've just lost your mom."

"We won't do it now. We'll wait until the time is right." Her eyes are wide, her pupils dilated.

I'd think my daughter was on drugs, except I know she's not. She's been at my wife's side for days while we waited for the end. She was there in the months my wife was delusional before she died, while Wilma forgot who she was and where we were.

She forgot all of us. She'd felt like she was losing her

mind and, in turn, Holly and I felt the same. Now, though, my daughter isn't covered in the mantle of grief she's felt since losing her mom. She's not high on anything but the idea of hurting the man who took her mom from her.

"When the time is right, we can talk about it," I tell her, hoping I can offer her this small olive branch and that she'll forget about it in time. I'm too sad to be angry right now, too broken. I just want my wife back and don't have the energy to try to hurt the man who took her from us.

"Promise?"

I nod. "Promise." Even as I make this promise to my daughter, I'm not sure it's the right thing to do. I feel her anger running through me, but it hasn't had time to take root and grow like it has in her. Surely, with the passing of time, we'll both find peace, not more anger.

Right?

I think about looking my wife's killer in the eyes and telling him I forgive him. I think about what it would be like to give him that gift of peace and let him know that all is forgotten.

I don't think I can do that.

The anger is taking root.

I try to imagine shaking his hand and letting him know it's all okay, that Holly and I are okay, that life has moved on without my wife.

I feel it coiling deeper in me.

I wonder what it would be like to see him suffer the way I'm suffering, for him to see his wife slowly lose her mind until she finally goes. To know that the person he loved more than anything in the world is dead because of someone else's actions.

· · ·

THEN I LOOK at my daughter, who is staring at me with the same trusting expression she wore on her face when she was a little girl. Holly always knew I would fix whatever problem we ran into. She knew I would handle anything bad that happened and that I would right wrongs.

And it's right now that I know, without a doubt, that given the chance, I'd like to make my wife's killer suffer.

Wilma wouldn't want this. She would want us to forgive and let him live his life. She'd say that it was an honest mistake, that we shouldn't let it tear us apart from the inside. My wife would demand that I forgive him and make me promise not to hurt him. She didn't want to see more suffering in the world, didn't want to think about people hurting unnecessarily.

But my wife isn't here anymore, is she.

1

AMY

Yanking the house keys from my pocket, I jangle them at my husband. "Welcome home," I crow, then fit the key into the lock. Leaning into it, I cram it into the keyhole and twist it hard to the side. There's a slight pause, and at first I'm sure it's not going to open, but then the door gives a low moan as it swings in.

"Home sweet home," Tim remarks, glancing over my shoulder into the house. "How long did the Realtor say this place has been empty?"

"Years." I knock a spiderweb out of the way and step confidently into the house, not wanting Tim to know that I'm a little nervous about what we're going to find here. This is a good thing. The two of us need a fresh start, and what better way to get one than to physically move to a new place? "The last owners were really old, it fell into disrepair, and it's a small town in Tennessee. Add all those up and it explains why we were able to get it for such a good price."

"A really good price," Tim agrees, reaching out and rubbing his hand on the wall before flicking the light switch, "but I'm sure we're going to be putting more than our fair share of work into the place."

A single bare bulb hanging from the middle of the foyer ceiling flickers and then turns on, casting a sad ring of light around us.

"I bet a chandelier there would look amazing," I say, pointing up. "Can you imagine how great this place is going to look after we have taken care of it?"

"It's going to be incredible." Tim puts his suitcase down just inside the front door and glances around the space.

His jaw is tight, and I know it's because he's not totally sure if this house is the right move for us, but I am. I couldn't stay one more night in our old apartment knowing what had happened there. Tim promised me it was a one-time thing with someone from work and I believe him. She's moved on to a new job and he and I have the fresh start we deserve.

Pushing the thoughts about Tim's affair from my mind, I look around the house.

From here we can take the curving staircase up to the second floor, the door on the right into the kitchen, or the door on the left into the living room. There's even a third door under the staircase, and I walk right up to it, running my hands over the outline as I look for a knob.

"I feel like we're in a game show," Tim says, pushing open a door before poking his head into the kitchen. "Which door do you want to open? Door number one?" He spins around and points at the door to the living room. "Door number two?" With a flourish, he gestures to the kitchen door. "Or door number three?" Now he comes up next to me and taps lightly on the door under the staircase.

"I want door number three," I tell him, stepping back and putting my hands on my hips. "But I don't know if that's going to happen."

"Weird. Was it on the plans the Realtor gave us?"

I shake my head. "But remember they were old. She even said there was a chance the last owners did some upgrades that might not be listed. You'd think the family would disclose that when putting the house up for sale, but maybe the bank didn't know. I mean, they foreclosed on it, so who knows what kind of stuff went on in here."

"Huh." He taps on the door once more and then shrugs. "We could stand here all day long trying to figure it out, or we can do some more exploring. What do you think?"

I think exploring sounds great, and I tell him that. It was a huge leap of faith for us to buy this house without actually viewing it in person, but we were afraid someone else would swoop in and grab it before we could, so we put in an offer the day it went on the market. I know I'm the one who really pushed for it, but I couldn't help myself.

Who doesn't want a huge old house with sprawling gardens, a koi pond, and acres of woods to explore? Sure, everything is in dire need of repair, and we're going to have to do most of the work ourselves to afford it all, but I'm secretly hoping Tim will be cool with us hiring a gardener.

He knows I love gardening, but I'm not the one to get gardens looking their best. If we could hire someone to help manage things and wrangle back the vines and weeds, then we'll have this place back to its prime in no time, and I think I could stay on top of maintenance.

The parties we're going to host here will be epic. We got this house for a song, and I know most of our friends paid the same price for small townhouses.

"It's wild that we were able to get the house so cheap, isn't it?" I can't help the squeal in my voice as Tim leads us into the kitchen. This time, when he flicks the switch, huge lights come on immediately, bathing us and the largest prep space I've ever seen in bright light. "How did we get so lucky?"

"I have no idea." I'm listening to him but already throwing

open cupboards and looking inside. It's not like I'm expecting to find anything, but it's still fun to explore. In addition to plenty of cupboard and counter space, there's a huge walk-in pantry and an island with cupboards on all four sides. Right here in the kitchen is exactly where I'd like a landline just in case our cell service isn't good, but Tim already told me he thought that was a silly expense to pay for, so I push that thought from my mind.

Across the room there's a door with a small latch on it. Flipping the latch open, I turn and grin at my husband. "Just another pantry, you think?" Cold air washes over me when I open the door and peer into the inky black.

"That's creepy," Tim says. "Must be the root cellar." He walks across the kitchen to stand next to me for a moment, looping his arm around my waist.

I agree, pushing the door closed and throwing the latch on it. It cuts off the cool air, and I nod, looking up at him. "When we have the gardens up and running, it'll be great to have some storage space. We're so far from town I don't really want to be running to the shops every single time we need something like an onion or a potato."

"Aren't you just a regular Laura Ingalls Wilder?" he asks, pulling me to him and giving me a kiss. "I had no idea you were so salt of the earth when I married you."

"That's because we've only been married two weeks." I kiss him back and then step backwards. "Speaking of which, I wanted to thank you for being okay with us using the money from your parents for the down payment on this place instead of on a honeymoon. This is going to last so much longer."

"One day you owe me a scuba diving trip. That's my concession. When you're a big-time author bringing in the big bucks, I want an awesome vacation." He smiles, but there's an edge to his voice.

"You got it." Grinning, I grip his arm and then turn to look around the kitchen. "When I'm a rich author, maybe you can quit your job. What do you say?"

"I say I won't miss HR one bit. Ready to keep exploring?"

He only had to ask once, and I was leading the way through the rest of the first floor. The house is amazing, although it is in serious need of redecorating. Besides the poor lighting in the foyer, there's old wallpaper on most of the walls that I can't wait to start ripping down, and I pluck at a loose seam as we explore the rest of the house.

There's already some furniture in here, including rocking chairs on the front porch and a dining table that has definitely seen better days. I drag my finger through the dust on the table before we walk back to the stairs.

The stairs are wide and curved, and I run my hand along the smooth banister as we make our way to the second floor. "There are three bedrooms up here," I say to Tim, turning to face him at the top of the stairs, "which means plenty of room for kids. And two bathrooms and even a small office, which is where I'll set up shop for writing."

"You don't want to write in the first-floor office off the living room?" He follows me down the hall as I throw open doors to the various bedrooms, all of them empty.

When we get to the small room that I'll be using as an office, I grab his hand and pull him in after me. "Not a chance. The Realtor said this room had a great view, and I've been dying to see if she was right. Let's check it out."

I push an old curtain out of the way, and Tim and I stare out the window. From here we can see the rest of the property, including the gardens that are in such need of work. According to the information the Realtor gave us, there's a fountain hidden somewhere in the thick brush below the window. There are also paths winding through the gardens and into the woods, but we can't see them right now.

Everything is so overgrown that I can only imagine the amount of work it's going to take to bring this place back to its prior glory.

"I didn't know there was a small building on the property," Tim says, pointing out the window.

I follow the line of his finger and frown, trying to see exactly what he's pointing at. "Where?" Shifting position, I peer through another pane, but not before I reach up and use the sleeve of my hoodie to wipe away some of the grime on the glass. This house is gorgeous, but dirty, and I can only imagine what some vinegar and elbow grease will do to the glass.

"There. Past that big hedgerow. I'm pretty sure I can see a roof. Do you see it? It's the patch of brown right in the middle of all the green."

Frowning, I peer harder. "I think I see it," I say, using my hand to block out some of the sun's glare. "Oh, yeah! What is that?"

Tim shrugs. "I have no idea. Did you see anything about a shed on the property plans?"

"No, and that looks bigger than just a shed," I say, glancing at it once more before pulling my phone from my pocket. "Surely there's some information from the Realtor, right? Like a disclosure document? I can't imagine there would be a building on the property that we don't know about."

"Sure, but you know places like this," Tim says, putting his arm around me and guiding me away from the window. "The place hasn't been occupied in years, and I bet documents got lost. But we should check it out. Maybe the owners didn't get a building permit for it, and that's why it's not on the paperwork."

I frown. "Does that mean we're going to have to pay taxes on it?"

"No idea, but I'm not going to worry about it." He pulls me closer to him and kisses the tip of my nose. "I'm pretty sure there's something else I'd much rather be doing in our new house right now. What do you say?"

"Sounds good to me," I tell him, grinning back at him. We swapped our honeymoon for this place, and as soon as Tim goes back to work, I'm not going to see him much at all. I might as well enjoy myself before he gets busy again.

This is good. It's our fresh start. We can make this work, no matter what we have to overcome. We've already been through so much that there's no reason why we can't enjoy this second chance and come out stronger than ever.

This is the right move. I know it.

Even as I think that, though, I can't stop wondering about that strange little building.

2

TIM

I know Amy hasn't stopped thinking about the little building on the property, but all it's done since we moved in is rain. The last thing we wanted to do was go for a wet walk through the overgrown gardens to explore the building. Amy had reached out to Holly, our Realtor, to see if she knew anything about the strange building, but over breakfast this morning, Amy told me she hadn't heard back from Holly.

"Are you totally sure you don't want to wait for me to get home?" I'm at my desk, and I cradle the phone against my shoulder so I can quickly respond to an email I just got. "I know you're antsy, Amy, but the building isn't going anywhere anytime soon. It's not like it's going to get up and walk away, and I'll be finished here in about half an hour."

"But it's not raining for the first time since we spotted it," she counters. "I found some old clippers in the storage shed by the house and thought I'd try to whack a path through the garden to see what it is. Do you really want me to wait for you?"

"You don't have to." I press send, then give Amy my full

attention again. "I just know you were worried yesterday about what you might find out there."

"That was after two glasses of wine," she points out. "And I doubt there will be anything more than a family of raccoons, if that." She pauses, and I can just picture her standing by the front door as she gazes out at the yard. "Do you not think it's a good idea?"

"No, no, I think it's fine." The truth is that I want to be there to make sure there isn't a rabid dog or something living in the building. I do think it's a bit strange that we don't have any information about it being built, but I'm probably just being paranoid. "I love you, and I'll be home as soon as possible, okay?"

"Love you! I'll send you pictures if I find anything good. Don't forget pizza on your way home, okay?"

"You got it," I tell her, grinning as we both hang up. I navigate to the county's website to study the overview of our property while I mull over the conversation we just had. The website hasn't been updated in two decades, and the small building isn't there.

I'm dying of curiosity and wish that Amy had waited for me to join her so I could see the building too, but I'll have to check it out later.

Just because she gets to see it first doesn't mean it'll be any less cool by the time I get to see it.

Man, I love my wife. Amy is everything to me. I almost lost her once, and I'm not about to do that again. The fact that she forgave me for the affair I had before we got married speaks to what an amazing woman she just is.

She's smart and funny and sassy, and if she wants to explore the property without me, then of course I'm okay with it. I just want to be there with her, and for her, always. I promised Amy I would never make the same mistake again, and I meant it.

It was a big switch for us to move from our little apartment downtown to this house in the middle of nowhere, and I want to make sure everything is perfect.

Amy had been hunting for our ideal home for months before we got married, and the hunt only intensified after my stupid mistake. She'd been posting in the local Facebook group about her house hunting, and when a Realtor reached out with this one, I couldn't say no. She called the Realtor who'd tagged her in the post about the house, and the next thing I knew, we'd put in an offer. Sure, I'm not so keen on the fact that we don't have any neighbors within shouting distance, but, as Amy pointed out, it was a much better alternative to listening to our upstairs neighbors sweeping the floor after dinner.

After the little old couple above us moved out and the young couple with toddler twins moved in, I agreed with Amy. We'd lived together for a few years before getting married, and I knew deep in my heart that we wouldn't ever be really happy if we didn't have a place of our own.

Of course, I wasn't expecting our place to be a sprawling estate with ivy crawling up the exterior walls and wide floorboards that probably need sanding and refinishing, but my wife is happy, so I'm happy.

That's what my dad always told me when I was younger. Happy wife, happy life. And after what I did, Amy deserves whatever she wants if it'll make her happy.

"You busy?" My boss, Marie, leans in the doorway, holding her coffee mug, rapping on the door to get my attention while she speaks.

"Nope." I shake my head to clear it and click away from the satellite view of our new house and pull up my email like I was working on that.

"Great." Marie sits across from me and takes a sip of her coffee.

It's almost four in the afternoon, but I have a strong suspicion that she's still drinking proper coffee. It would have kept me up all night. I have to switch to decaf after my first cup in the morning, but Marie operates on a different level to most people I've ever met.

"I want to talk to you about your position here," she continues.

Now my palms grow sweaty. It doesn't usually bother me when she pops in to say something, but now, for some reason, I start reflecting on all the things I might have done wrong in this job. We just bought the house, and right now is definitely not the time to lose my job. "My position?"

"Yep." She takes a long sip and pulls her reading glasses from the top of her head. Perching them on her nose, she stares at me over them before thumbing on her phone. "You've been with us for four years. Is that correct?"

I nod. "Since right out of college, yes."

"Great, I thought you joined us right away. In that time you've gone to a number of continuing education conferences and meetings, consistently exceeded expectations for your position, and you're always here on time. I like that, Tim."

"Thanks." I'm still not sure where this is going. My phone vibrates in my pocket, and I bet it's Amy sending pictures of the little building on the property. As much as I want to look at them, I have to ignore them for now.

"We'd like to offer you a raise," Marie says, finally putting her phone down on my desk. "As you know, TechCorp is expanding, and we're looking to hire two new HR reps who will be in our satellite offices. You'll be in charge of them. We also want you to handle the hiring and firing for our company, which will take all that off my plate. What do you think?"

This is not what I was expecting when she appeared in my doorway, and I can't help the grin that spreads across my face. "Seriously? Marie, that sounds great! What does that mean for my schedule?"

"Same hours." She stands up, flapping her hand at me. "I know you're recently married, so I wouldn't want to take you away from home. Of course, there will be mandatory training sessions you'll have to attend, but you'll be paid for them. I think you'll go far with our company if you're willing to invest the time and effort."

"Excellent." I'm almost giddy now and trying to hold back my excitement so she doesn't realize how thrilled I am. Sure, Amy and I sacrificed our honeymoon for the house, and I make enough money to pay for it, but any raise I get will not only make our lives more comfortable, but it will also pay for the renovations and repairs we need to make on the house.

And I know Amy's ready to start trying for kids, and they're really expensive. It's best if we start putting money aside now for expenses before we're neck-deep in paying for diapers. This raise means Amy can start putting all her income into savings for our future kids.

"Great. I had a feeling you'd agree. Congratulations, Tim. And I'll be in touch with the dates for the continuing education classes, okay? Keep an eye on your email, and I'll get that information to you as soon as possible."

"Sounds great, thanks." I give her another huge grin and manage to wait until she's left my office before pulling my phone from my pocket. My first thought is to text Amy right away, but then I stop. Maybe it would be more fun to tell her over dinner. I know I'm supposed to pick up a pizza, but steak and twice-baked potatoes from the classy place on the way home seems like a nicer celebration meal.

I'm sure Amy won't mind. Instead of sharing my good news, I turn on my phone and flick through to the messages she sent me. I was right—they were taken as she walked through the garden to the little building. There's a lot of thick weeds she had to wade through, and then a picture of the building.

It's a little house. At least, that's exactly what it looks like to me, like someone built a tiny little country house right off to the side of our garden, but that doesn't make any sense. Wait—maybe it's a caretaker's cottage. I've heard of this role before. When someone owns too large a property to manage the garden and grounds on their own, they hire someone to live on the property and do it for them.

Excitement grows in me when I think about all the ways we can use this little house. Of course, even with my raise, I might not be able to pay someone to take care of the property full time, but this would be the perfect little writing retreat for Amy. Or I could finally pick up a guitar and amp like I keep saying I will and practice out in the garden.

There's a whole series of shots from the outside of the cottage, and I flick through them, growing more and more excited with each one. I hope Amy hasn't already claimed it for herself in her mind, because I can definitely see myself happily goofing about out there, as long as the inside isn't in terrible disrepair.

I've pretty much planned out exactly what I'll do to the inside of the cottage to make sure it fits my needs, when I flick to the last picture, and my heart stops.

The property seemed abandoned, so what I'm seeing doesn't make any sense.

3

AMY

I feel my heart pounding hard as I click off my phone's screen and put it in my pocket. I feel like I'm doing something illegal by entering this little cottage, but I have to remind myself it is on our property, and that means we own it.

I can go in if I want to. There isn't anything stopping me from opening the door and stepping inside, but after I sent Tim the pictures, I feel like I'm breaking and entering. That's because, unlike the rest of the property that is in disrepair and in need of some serious work, the inside of the cottage is in perfect condition.

Sure, the outside of it is covered with vines that need to be removed, and the windows definitely need as good a deep clean as the ones in the house, but the inside of the cottage honestly looks like someone was living here as recently as this morning.

There's a stack of books on the table along with a place setting, like someone's just popped to the store and will be back to make themselves something to eat in a few minutes.

A bookshelf by the little fireplace is loaded with more books and knickknacks, and the kitchen is spotless.

A neatly folded dry rag lies next to the sink, and when I turn in a complete circle, I see a perfectly made bed right by the front door. The cottage is only one small room with a bathroom attached, but it feels more homey and comfortable than any place I've ever been.

That might be due to the soft green color of the walls or the fact that all the dishes in the open shelving in the kitchen are mismatched and cute in their stacks of multiple colors. I don't know what it is about the cottage, but I instantly fall in love with it.

When my phone rings, I pull it from my pocket and answer without looking at the screen. I'm too busy staring around the cottage, turning in small circles on a handwoven rug, to worry about who's calling.

"How's it going, Amy?" Our Realtor's voice is cheery and bright, and I have to shake my head a little to focus on her and not on the cottage. "Get all settled in over the weekend? Need anything?"

"Oh, it's all great," I tell her, going to the door and stepping outside. "Seriously, we can't thank you enough for finding this place. I have no idea how you did it and how you were able to deal with the bank and get them to close so quickly, but we love it. It's amazing."

"I'm so glad! Well, I don't want to bother you, but I always like to check in on my buyers after they've had a little time to settle in their new home, and to make sure they don't need anything."

"One thing," I say, turning and looking back at the cottage as I close the door. It wasn't locked when I got here, and since I don't have a key, I don't want it to lock now accidentally, preventing entry for a while. I can only imagine how terrible I would feel if we had to break a window to get into the cottage. "What do you know about the little cottage by the gardens?"

"Little cottage?" she asks, then pauses.

My phone beeps in my ear, and I pull it away from my head to look at it. It's Tim, but he's going to have to wait until I get off the phone with Holly. I don't want to be rude.

"It's darling," I say, like that's going to jog her memory. "I had to come all the way through the gardens and almost to the woods to find it. We only noticed it when we were exploring the house. It's just visible from the little room I'm going to use for my office."

Holly chuckles. "I'm so sorry, but I can't picture what you're talking about. You'll have to send me a photo or something if you want more information."

"No, it's fine," I say, suddenly feeling silly. What does it matter if there is a little cottage here on the property that wasn't listed in the information about the house? This is what Tim and I get for not actually driving out here to look at it before putting in an offer and buying it. We were both just so excited about it from the pictures that we decided to buy it sight unseen.

Not that it was a mistake. Sure, it's a little weird that the cottage is here and in such great condition, but that's really not a big deal in the grand scheme of things. And Tim and I still haven't been able to get that door under the stairs open, but now I think I'd feel silly even mentioning it to Holly.

Doors stick. Houses settle, and I'm sure that's all that's going on.

"Okay, well, if there's anything else you two need, or if you know someone looking to buy or sell, please give them my name!" Her voice is rushed and sounds a little bit thicker than it did a moment ago. It's obvious she's ready to get off the phone. "It was such a pleasure working with you and Tim. Enjoy the house!"

"Thanks," I tell her, and then she hangs up. Weird that she abruptly ended our conversation like that, but I bet she had another call coming in. That reminds me, I missed a call from Tim. I dial him up, tapping my foot impatiently while the line rings and rings.

It clicks over to voicemail, and I sigh, but put a smile on my face before leaving my message.

"Hey, I missed you," I say, grabbing my clippers from where I'd put them on the ground outside the cottage. "Call me back, okay? Or I'll see you at dinner, either way."

It's not unheard of for Tim to not pick up when I call him. It seems like he's always putting out fires at work, which I guess is the nature of working in HR. I don't have to deal with other people when I'm working, which means not only can I pop out to the gardens when I want a little bit of an escape during the day, but I have to be on top of what I'm working on to make sure my articles get turned in on time.

Tim knows I'd much rather be an author than ghostwrite articles for various online companies, but at least the work is steady. It doesn't pay nearly as much as his HR job, but the little money I bring in will help pay for whatever work needs doing around here. And because I'm not chained to my desk all day long, I can take little breaks during the day to weed in the garden or whip up a batch of cookies so Tim has something delicious to come home to.

In fact, I think I'll bake some now. After putting the clippers back, I wander into the kitchen and wash my hands. From here I can see the garden, but it's so overgrown and the cottage is too far from the house to see it. As I get everything I need to bake out of the cupboards and turn on the oven, I can't help but wish I were baking in the little cottage instead.

It's just so cozy. I have no idea why it looks so nice compared to the rest of the property, but there was something about it that was comforting.

And then it hits me.

I'd been so charmed by the little cottage and so busy looking around at all the cute little touches, I hadn't paid attention to the cup of tea on the table.

I know it was tea, because there was a little plate with a teabag sitting on it right by the cup. There was a small spoon upturned on the plate like someone had used it to stir sugar into their tea.

I don't know why I didn't register the problem with all of that until now.

The tea had still been steaming.

4

TIM

I don't get a chance to call Amy again until five o'clock. Slamming my thumb onto the power button on my computer, I shut it down, grab my keys and water bottle, and hurry out of my office. Marie has strict rules about not making or taking personal calls during work hours, but I'd broken that rule earlier in the day when I reached out to Amy.

Not that I think she would catch me in the privacy of my office, but she's known to pop in to see what people are doing just to keep them on their toes. I didn't want her to find me on the phone and have to explain that right after the good news she gave me.

I ended up in the bathroom, trying to call my wife, which made me feel like I was in high school again, breaking the rules between classes. She hadn't picked up when I called and so far hasn't responded to my texts, so I dialed her number as I got in my car, tucking the phone against my shoulder as I backed out of my space.

"Amy," I say when she picks up on the first ring. "Hey, are you still in the cottage?"

"No." Her voice is tight, and I can picture her gripping the phone so hard her fingers go white. "No, I'm in the house. I was going to bake cookies, but then I realized something about the cottage."

"I know it sounds crazy, and it probably isn't true, but it looks like someone lives there," I say at the same time she says: "I think someone lives there."

Exhaling hard, I force myself to relax my grip on the steering wheel. My hand was already starting to cramp up, and I still have the long drive home before I can really relax. "Okay, I'm sure there's a reasonable explanation, honey. You still want me to stop and pick up dinner, or do you want me to get there sooner so we can call the police?"

She pauses, and I know she's trying to be brave. Amy hates it when she has to rely on other people for help, and I'm sure if I show up at home without dinner in hand, she's going to be ticked unless it's exactly what she wants me to do.

"Dinner, please," she says, sighing. "I was going to make some cookies so that the house would smell good when you got home, but I don't have anything to make for an actual meal. So unless you want chocolate chip cookies for dinner and dessert, better grab something. I'm starving." Her voice is small when she continues, "I never thought to call the police. I just wanted you home."

"It's okay," I tell her. "I don't know many people who would have been thinking straight in that situation. It's really weird." I slow to a stop at a red light even though all I want to do is slam down on the gas to get home to my wife as quickly as possible. "Stay in the house if you really want to wait until I get home, okay?"

"Don't worry, I locked the front door as soon as I got in. I don't know that anyone was actually there, Tim, but it's the weirdest thing. I swear the tea on the table was still hot."

That changes things. It's one thing for someone to have

been living on the property previously, but another entirely for them to still be there after we bought the house. "Amy, I want you to call the police, okay? Seriously. If someone is on the property, then they should know about it."

"You think so?" She suddenly sounds really scared, and I feel bad for doing that to her, but I don't like the thought that someone was at the cottage recently. "I don't want to get off the phone with you."

"Okay, that's fine." I press down harder on the gas, inching my speed up over the speed limit. If I do get pulled over, which I pray that I won't, I'll just explain what's going on. I can't imagine any police officer would detain me if they knew my wife was in the house scared about someone on the property.

"How was your day?" Amy's trying to fill the silence and make herself feel better.

It hits me that I have good news for my wife, and it's something that might take her mind off what's going on at the house. "I got a raise," I say, turning onto the main road that will lead me right by the pizza place and also the restaurant where I wanted to stop and get us something really nice to eat. My stomach growls, and I want to pull over, but I need to get home to Amy. We might not get a real dinner tonight, but we'll both survive. "And a promotion."

"Tim!" She squeals out my name, and I suddenly feel better about everything. Sure, I want to get home to her as quickly as possible so we can call the cops and figure all of this out, but we'll be fine.

"Your raise is really good news," she tells me, and I feel myself relax. As long as I stay on the phone with her, I can make sure nothing crazy happens. Yes, she's scared, and I'm worried, but we'll be just fine.

"It is," I tell her. "I was going to stop and grab some steak for dinner to celebrate. As soon as we have all this straightened out, I'm taking you out on the town. I'm talking your favorite dress, a suit for me, and all the steak and champagne we can handle."

She laughs, and I feel myself relax even more. Just a few more minutes on the road and I'll be pulling into our long driveway that winds up the side of the mountain to our home. It's so private up there, which is exactly what we wanted, but now it feels almost silly to live somewhere so isolated.

"Hey, I'm going into no-man's-land," I tell her, referring to the space between the main part of town and our home where there isn't any cell reception. The mountains here are snuggled so tightly together they make it impossible to make or receive calls for a stretch along the road. "Call the police so that they get there right after I do, okay? I love you, Amy."

"I love you." Her voice trembles, and I know she doesn't want to get off the phone, but we're about to get cut off in a moment anyway, so she really should go ahead and make the call. "See you so—"

And the call is dropped. I just want to get to my wife. Without glancing at my screen, I set my phone in my cup holder and drive faster. I want to eat up the space between the two of us even though I'm sure everything will be fine. Amy's locked in the house, and we're the only ones with keys. Nothing bad will happen to her.

I drive even faster.

5

AMY

I t felt ridiculous calling the police and explaining that I thought someone had been staying on our property, but either it was a really slow day for calls or they took me seriously, because a police car pulled up onto our driveway right behind Tim. I'd been watching from the front door, my hand resting on the doorknob so that I could rush to my husband as soon as he got home.

Even though I know the house is locked up tight and nobody can get in, I still felt like someone was watching me. It's just my nerves, I'm sure of that, but even knowing that my nerves are getting the best of me doesn't stop me from throwing the door open and rushing across the porch and the driveway to throw myself into Tim's arms.

Immediately, he wraps his arms around me and pulls me close. I feel myself sinking into his embrace and only pull back when an officer walks up to us.

"Mrs. Matthews?" he asks, glancing at me. "I'm Officer Allen. You're the one who made the call?"

I nod, pulling away from Tim so I can look at the man. He towers over both of us and obviously spends a lot of time at the gym. Instantly, I feel better about calling the police for help. Maybe it's silly, but the gun on his hip and the no-nonsense expression on his face makes me feel like he can handle anything we find in the cottage.

"I am," I say. "Thanks for coming."

"Not a problem. Now, dispatch said you think someone was living in your cottage?"

"*Is* living in our cottage," I correct him. "I went down there, and there was hot water in the teacup on the table."

"Lead the way," he says, letting his eyes skim over Tim.

"It's through the garden," I say, taking Tim's hand and pulling him after me. "We just moved in this weekend, so I'm sorry that it's kind of overgrown." I feel silly making this man follow me along a path you can barely see in the garden. Sure, I cut back a lot of vines that were encroaching on the path, but I'd been so excited to get to the cottage that I'd ignored most of them.

We pick our way through the garden, each of us stepping over plants that have thrown themselves across the path, until we finally reach the cottage.

"This is it," I say, gesturing nervously at the door. "I went in there, and it was pretty obvious someone is living there."

"You said there was hot tea on the table?"

I nod.

"And nobody has permission to be on your property?"

"That's correct." Tim speaks up, obviously wanting to get involved.

I squeeze his fingers. I know he feels bad that I had to handle all this on my own, but he's here now, and so is this officer. Things are going to be just fine, I know it.

"You two stay outside, and I'll have a look." The officer rests one hand on the grip of his gun and knocks on the door with the other. "Police," he calls. "I'm coming in." When he doesn't get a response, he pushes the door open, then leans in and looks around before entering the cottage.

Tim waits until he's inside, and then he turns to me, cupping my cheek in his hand. "I was worried about you," he says.

"I'm okay. I was pretty nervous, but I'm sure everything is fine. It was just ... why didn't I notice the tea when I was here? I feel stupid that it wasn't until I was back in the kitchen that I realized what was so wrong." I shake my head, not sure that I want to continue. I don't want to tell him that I felt like someone was watching me in the house.

That would only freak him out, and I really love it here. I loved it from the moment Holly sent me the listing and told us the bank might be willing to drop the price if we were willing to commit to a quick sale. Tim acquiesced because he could tell how much I loved this place, and I know I'm the one who likes it the most.

I don't want him to have any reason to dislike it.

"I don't see a teacup on the table," Officer Allen says, coming back out and eyeballing me. "Are you sure it was there?"

"I'm sure," I say, frowning; then it hits me. "Hold on, I took a picture of the inside of the cottage! I bet you can see it there." I fumble my phone from my pocket and flip through the pictures I took until I find the one I'm looking for, but when I look at it, my heart sinks. "Never mind, I didn't get the table in the picture."

Officer Allen gives a small chuckle. "Moving is stressful. I'd wager a bet you're a little tired, am I right?"

I nod, feeling my face flush. *He doesn't believe me.* The thought hits me, and I swallow hard, trying to choke down some of my disappointment. "I'm tired, sure, but I know what I saw."

"But you have no proof." He gives me what I think is his

best, kind smile, but I can't help but think there's a little condescension under it. "Mrs. Matthews, sometimes, when we're tired, we think we see things that aren't really there. I bet you thought you saw it because the inside of the cottage is so well kept."

We're all silent, and I know the officer wants me to agree with him, but that's the last thing I want to do. I know what I saw, even though he doesn't believe me. He wasn't here, anyway, so I'm not surprised he thinks I'm crazy. The cup of tea isn't here now, and there isn't any proof that it ever was.

Ignoring both him and Tim, I push past them and walk into the cottage. The air smells clean in here, but there isn't a whiff of tea. I go over to the sink and look in it, almost like I expect the cup or spoon to be sitting in there, but the sink is empty. If the cup was washed and put back on the shelf, they must have wiped the sink, as there isn't a drop of water.

I glance along the open shelves past the plates and bowls, until I see the glasses and then the little teacups. The one I swear was on the table is there now, the tiny vines and little purple violets around the outside a pattern I wouldn't soon forget.

Reaching up, I lightly touch it. I don't know what I'm expecting, but I guess I'm half-hoping it will still be warm. It's not, though, and I feel my shoulders slump in disappointment as I turn back to the small door and watch my husband talking to the officer.

"Thanks for coming out," Tim says, shaking the officer's hand. "We appreciate how quickly you got here."

"Not a problem." The officer flashes my husband a smile he hadn't given me. "Like I said, moving is stressful, and to come live in a place this isolated and empty ... well, I can imagine your mind would play tricks on you. You two feel free to call me if you need anything, okay?"

My husband says something else I don't quite catch; then

when the officer turns to leave, he comes into the cottage to talk to me, his head on a swivel as he looks around the space. I ignore him until he wraps his arms around me and buries his face in my neck.

"Are you okay?"

I shrug, wanting him to know I'm not happy but also not willing to push his arms off me. "I'm fine," I tell him. "But I promise you it was here." I gestured to the cottage. "I'm never coming in here again, believe me. Besides, isn't it weird that the cottage is set up so perfectly, like someone is living here, yet the main house is an absolute wreck?"

"Sure, but maybe the prior owners didn't have the ambition to clean the house. We don't know why they left it the way they did, Amy. Remember, the bank owned it. That means it was foreclosed on, so why would they care if the house and gardens looked a mess?"

"But you believe me, right? I thought you were a little bit worried before, but now you seem ..." I turn in his arms to look at him.

"Listen, it's weird, okay? But the teacup isn't on the table, and there's no indication that it ever was."

"Except for the fact that I saw it," I point out.

"So you're saying someone saw you come in here, then came back after you'd left and washed the cup and put it away, then disappeared before you had a chance to see them?"

My mouth drops open, and I have to force myself to shut it. He thinks I'm making all this up, I'm sure of it.

But I'm not, I swear I'm not. "I didn't see anyone," I admit. I still don't want to tell him that I felt someone watching me earlier when I was waiting for him to get home. He'd probably think I'd gone right off the deep end and wonder what in the world the two of us got ourselves into by buying this place.

"Okay." He kisses my forehead, then takes my hand to lead me to the door. "Then why don't you and I go up to the house and get changed for dinner? I really want to take you out to celebrate."

"I want pizza." It probably sounds silly, but right now the last thing I want to do is leave the house. Sure, I swear I felt someone watching me here, but this is our home. I don't want to turn tail and run just because I'm a little bit freaked out. "Can't we order it and have it delivered?"

He laughs, the sound so bright and loud it chases away any fears I'm fighting. "Amy, that sounds like a dream, but I think we left delivery behind us when we moved here. I can't imagine what the bill would be to have some poor delivery driver find us, navigate the driveway, and not drive off into the woods if it's dark by the time they arrive."

"But you're okay with us navigating the driveway in the dark?" It's silly, but I'm suddenly worried by that very prospect.

Tim leads me through the garden, and I pick my way around a rose bush I should have trimmed back when I was out here earlier.

"Darling," he tells me, helping me over the thorns, "I won't let anything happen to you, okay? You just have to trust me."

I do trust him. That's not the problem.

The problem is that I don't think my husband believes a word I've just said.

6

TIM

I know Amy is still a little freaked out by the possibility someone could have been in the little cottage on our property earlier this week, but I can't worry about that. No one was there, and even if there had been, they're long gone now. I know she keeps peeking out the window when she thinks I'm not looking in the evenings, but there's nothing to see except for an overgrown yard and a small cottage that looks like it was designed in fairy-tale land.

That's why I'm tackling the garden this weekend. I'm up and dressed for it already before she even comes downstairs, my arms and legs protected by long sleeves and heavy jeans. I'm sure it was the smell of coffee that pulled her from her slumber, so I pour her a cup and hand it to her before topping mine up and leaning against the counter to talk to her.

"You look like a lumberjack," she remarks, throwing me a wink as she takes a sip of her coffee. "But I like it, don't get me wrong."

"Do you, now? Good to know." I grin at her. Even with extreme bedhead, my wife is gorgeous. She grips the coffee mug like it's the only thing keeping her alive. "I know you've been busy with writing this week, but have you had time to get into the garden at all?"

Amy shakes her head slowly, which I already knew she was going to do. There's a pile of stripped wallpaper in the hall outside our bedroom door, and her office looks perfectly set up, but I had a pretty good feeling she hadn't thought once about setting foot in the garden since she got so creeped out in the cottage.

I do my best to hide my frustration. Her getting out for little bits during the day to work in the garden was part of the plan all along. If she's not holding up her end of the bargain, then I have no idea how we're going to get this place looking better than it does right now.

"I've been working inside," she says, a defensive tone in her voice. "I hope that's okay."

"It's perfect." I don't want to remind her we'd agreed she'd spend as much time as possible in the garden before the weather turned nasty. It's obvious she wants to avoid it as much as possible, and my bringing it up is only going to upset her. Choosing my next words carefully, I do my best to diffuse the dark look on her face. "I love the work you're doing. I just want to tackle the yard before it totally engulfs the house."

This makes her brighten up, and she puts her mug down. "I'll change and help you, how does that sound?"

"Perfect. Don't you want breakfast first?"

She groans and shakes her head, standing and rubbing her stomach. "After that dinner last night? Not a chance. I think I ate my weight in steak and béarnaise sauce. Who knew how good it could be?"

"Me," I tell her, laughing as I take our mugs to the sink. "That's why I wanted to take you out and not just grab a pizza after the cops left. I know yesterday was stressful, but I think going out salvaged it, and we got to celebrate my raise." Rinsing the mugs quickly, I put them in the dishwasher. "Why don't you go ahead and change, then meet me out there? I'll start tackling the weeds that try to trip me every single time I walk to the car."

"Sounds perfect." She wiggles her fingers at me and disappears.

A moment later, I hear her running up the stairs, and I head outside. The morning is crisp and cool, the perfect weather for a little sweating in the yard, and I can't wait to see how much work we can get done before lunch. If the weather holds and we work hard, then I bet we can make quite a dent in the landscaping before we have to stop.

When Amy finally joins me outside, I already have on the thick leather gloves we bought after we closed on the house. The briars I'm wrangling from the walk by the house have to be as thick as my pinkie finger, but rather than just cutting them back, I'm doing my best to pull them out from the root.

"Let me help you." Amy dons her gloves, and together the two of us yank and pull, slowly working our way down the path.

It's hard going, and I leave her after an hour to get the wheelbarrow I saw leaning up against the side of the house.

The wheel is a little flat, and the entire thing looks like it might fall apart if I drive it over a rock, but it's what we have for now, and I make a mental note to buy a new one. It takes me longer to get back to where we were working than I would have liked because one of the wooden handles feels slightly rotten, and I have to keep adjusting my grip on it so that the entire thing doesn't fall apart.

When I get back, I see Amy standing right where I left her, her hand clamped over her calf, her face tight when she looks up at me. "A briar caught me and ripped right through my jeans."

"Oh! Are you okay?" Leaving the wheelbarrow where it is, I hurry to my wife and drop down to my knees in front of her. Her jeans are red and wet from where the briar snagged her. "Move your hand, honey. Let me see."

"I don't think it's bad," Amy says, letting go of her calf. "I just didn't want to go into the house without telling you first."

"You're okay," I say, eyeballing the ripped fabric. "There's a lot of blood, but I think you're going to be fine. Let's get you in there and clean it up, shall we?"

"I got it under control." She wipes her bloody hand on her jeans and gives me her best smile. "Really, Tim, it's going to be fine. I'm just gonna go bandage it up and change out of my jeans. Maybe this afternoon or tomorrow we can go shopping, what do you say? I think I'm going to need something a little more heavy duty."

"Carhartts," I say, nodding. "Me too. And a wheelbarrow. We'll get what we need, okay? Don't worry."

"Not worried," she calls over her shoulder as she walks up to the house. "We got this!"

Her optimism is inspiring, but I can't help but wonder if she's right. Moving here sounded great and looked amazing on paper, but I'm beginning to wonder if we might have bitten off a little more than we can chew. Even if I had mentioned my concerns to her before the move, though, I'm not sure I could have told her I didn't want to buy the house.

She wanted it, and after everything that had happened, I didn't feel like I had much of a choice in the matter. Now that we're here, though, we have a lot of work to do. Not only did we not come with any of the yard equipment we'll need to take care of this place, but most of what's already here is falling apart.

I can just see the dollar signs in my mind as I try to think about the long list of things we're going to have to buy. New clothes for working outdoors, a wheelbarrow, weed eater, mower ... it's overwhelming, at best.

But this is what Amy really wants, and I want to do what it will take to make her dream come true. Sure, I got the raise, and it's a good one, but I'd hate to spend all our money on equipment for the yard, especially when this is a lot harder than I thought it would be.

It sounds silly, but in my mind I'd had a relaxing mental image of pulling weeds after breakfast on Saturday while Amy cut fresh flowers from the garden. It was easy to imagine how wonderful it would be to have dinner parties so everyone could see how amazing our house looked.

But the reality is much more daunting. We're going to be out here every spare second of our lives working to make the yard and gardens look nice, especially if Amy doesn't want to work out here on her own because she's afraid someone else is around. Every single evening after work will be dominated by me pulling weeds and cutting back overgrown flowers and bushes.

Wiping my brow, I look up at the house. It towers over me, one side completely encased in ivy, which we both thought was charming until we learned it can structurally damage the house. All of it will need to be pulled, and then we might have to make repairs to keep the walls nice and sound.

This simply isn't going to work. We're going to have to get some help. I know Amy and I thought we could do it all on our own, but we can't. There's just no way we can handle all this work, not with me working full time and her trying to take her writing career to the next level.

We need help.

We need a caretaker.

Holly suggested it once before, and I'd written it off, but it's perfect. Not only will we have someone around who can do the majority of the hard work in the gardens, but Amy should feel a lot safer knowing there's someone around making sure no one else is skulking around the little cottage.

I bet, rather than asking someone to just come work during the day, we could offer for them to live on the property. That was how it was done in the past, right? A caretaker would move in, take care of the gardens, and in return have a place to live.

Surely it can't be that expensive, not when you factor in the free place to live. Whatever it costs, I'm willing to pay it if it means I don't have to spend all my free time doing the work myself. According to the paperwork Marie gave me this week on my new position, my raise is going to be enough to cover this.

Feeling better about the entire situation since I pulled my first briar this morning, I walk back up the path to the house, past the pile of briars and the wheelbarrow.

Amy is going to love this idea, I just know it. We'll have more free time to spend together, and she won't have to worry about someone creeping around the property since we'll have someone living here to help us keep an eye on the place.

I'm halfway up the steps to the porch when I hear her scream.

7

AMY

Two screams.

That's how long it takes for Tim to come flying into the kitchen, his eyes wide like he's just seen a ghost, his cheeks flushed from running.

My leg is all bandaged up. It didn't take long to find the first aid kit where I'd stashed it under the sink when we moved in, and clean up the wound before putting on some shorts. I'm done working in the garden today even though I know there's still a lot more work that needs doing.

It's not the fact that my leg still hurts that made me scream. It's the small teacup that my fingers brushed against when I opened the cupboard to get a glass for water. I almost didn't see it there, and then suddenly my fingers were running across the thin china, the little purple violets bright against the white background.

That's why I screamed.

"What is it?" Tim grabs my arm and turns me to face him.

I know he's worried that I'm physically hurt, but this is worse. The shock of what I've just seen in the cupboard numbs the dull burning ache in my leg.

"The teacup," I say, trying to make myself sound as calm and reasonable as possible. I know full well Tim is going to think I've lost my mind if I scream again, especially now that he knows that my leg injury isn't too bad. "It's the teacup from the cottage."

"The what now?" Frowning, Tim looks over to the open cupboard. I hadn't even closed it, I was so upset, and now the teacup is in full view like an accusation. "What are you talking about?"

I swallow hard to try to get my nerves under control. If there's one thing I know about my husband, it's that he doesn't like it when someone is hysterical. Few things irritate him more than not being able to talk to a person rationally. Maybe that's why he's so good at his job.

"That teacup," I say, swallowing again and pointing, "was in the cottage. It's the one that had the hot tea in it."

"This one? Are you sure?"

"Don't touch it!" I cry, reaching for his hand as he grabs the cup and turns to hold it out to me.

At my cry, Tim's eyes go wide, and I watch in horror as his fingers open, just a little, just enough for the cup to slip from his grasp. It falls to the ground, shattering on the tile floor between us.

"Oh, crap. I'm so sorry, Amy."

Ignoring him, I drop to my knees. Only shards remain, and I have a feeling there's no way we'd ever be able to put the teacup back together. I want to call the police, to let Officer Allen know we have proof. I want him to come with his fingerprint kit and dust the teacup for prints, as crazy as that sounds.

"What were you saying about it being in the cottage?" He lightly touches me on the shoulder. I hear the worry in his voice, and I close my eyes for just a moment to gather my thoughts.

Exhaling hard, I stand, then wipe my hands on my shorts. "That teacup," I say, gesturing to the pieces of china, "was on the cottage table on Monday with hot tea in it."

He stares at me. "Then how did it get into our cupboard?"

"Did you put it there?" It feels silly to ask him that, but I have to know. "Did you find it at the cottage and bring it home?"

He shakes his head. "Why in the world would I do that? And when would I have had the time? There's no way I would sneak around to move a teacup, Amy; think about it."

"But how did it get here, then?"

"It had to have been in the cupboard when we moved in, but we never really noticed. I know I haven't kept track of what dishes and other stuff were in the house when we got here. Have you?"

"No, but I promise you, it was in the cottage."

Silence grows between us, and I feel desperate, but I hold my ground.

Finally, right when I'm about to reach my breaking point, Tim sighs and runs his hand through his hair, pushing it back from his face. "Okay, Amy, I think we're both pretty stressed out about everything, wouldn't you agree?"

Stressed out is putting it mildly, but I know Tim. If it can't be proven with facts and figures, then it might as well never have happened. "Okay." Crossing my arms, I ignore the china pieces on the floor and lean against the counter. "What are you stressed out about?"

"The house? The garden? The fact that it took us all morning to rip up just a few briars and you got injured in the process? I feel like there's a fair amount to be stressed out about, don't you?"

"Sure. What should we do about it, though? And what should we do about the teacup? Please don't tell me you think I need to just get over it, that it was all in my head."

"No, no, nothing like that." He gently places his hands on my hips and pulls me closer until I'm snuggled up against him. "I think you're tired, and I'm tired. One of us had to have put the teacup there and not even realized what we were doing, okay? It was probably me. I'd bet you anything I found the teacup somewhere else and thought I'd put it where it belonged, but I never imagined it would freak you out. I'm so sorry, Amy."

"It's okay." His explanation and apology makes me snuggle even closer to him. "I probably overreacted; it was just such a shock to see it here."

"I bet. Okay, that's settled. I'm the mysterious teacup mover."

I laugh, and he kisses me.

"And I have a great idea. Hear me out." He looks excited, and I pull back to get a better look at his face. "I'm getting this great raise, right? And what better to spend our money on than peace of mind?"

"I'm listening, although I think a trip to Paris or London would be a really good thing to spend our money on too."

"That'll happen, I promise. I was thinking about something that will make our day-to-day life a little easier. I want to hire a caretaker for the property. Holly suggested it might be a good idea for the future, and I think she's right. There's just no way we can handle everything on our own, but if we hire someone, then the house will look amazing, and we'll still have free time to enjoy ourselves."

My mouth falls open, and I'm about to say something—although I don't know what yet—but Tim keeps talking.

"They can live in the cottage and not only clean up the garden, but give you peace of mind that someone is around and looking out for you. That way you don't have to worry about any intruders."

My mouth snaps shut as I try to think of what to say to him. It's not that I think it's a terrible idea, exactly, it's just …

"You hate it." Tim looks disappointed.

"No, I don't hate it," I say, holding back my response while I try to figure out exactly how I do feel about it. "It's not that at all. I'm just surprised, that's all. We talked about doing the majority of the work ourselves, and hiring someone to do it for us is a huge commitment."

"Not as huge as trying to put in hours of work every single day, Amy. Trust me, I would love it if the two of us could handle the gardens and grounds on our own, but look at what we've achieved today. It's not much."

"I know, but that was the dream."

He grabs my hands and squeezes them. "Dreams can change. There's absolutely nothing wrong with that. I'm fine with our dream changing a little bit if it means we can actually enjoy living here and not feel like we're constantly fighting the property. What do you say we do a trial run?"

"That sounds okay." A trial run would give us the chance to see if paying someone to take care of the property really was that good an idea, without the huge commitment that would make me feel bad if we decided not to keep the person on permanently. "One month? I have no idea how long you do a trial run like that for."

"Probably a month." He lets go of one of my hands and scratches his chin. "I'll just reach out to Holly, what do you say? See if she knows anyone who could do the job for us?"

"I think that's a good idea," I tell him, one hundred percent on board. I want to get the house and grounds in great condition, and, quite honestly, this place needs a lot more help than what I think the two of us can do on our own.

Part of me thought I could handle more. Honestly, I had this great mental image of me out here working in the garden, picking flowers, and showing off the work I did alongside the gardener.

But maybe that's not possible. I mean, look at the way the briar ripped through my jeans like they weren't even there. "Do you think we'll still have to buy all the stuff the caretaker needs? Lawn mower, weed eater, that sort of thing?"

He frowns. "It's not like we're going to look for a traditional lawn and garden crew, so I'd imagine so. I can't imagine someone just having all the tools and being willing to move in with it all to work for us, but I'll ask Holly. There's no doubt in my mind she'll know someone, okay? And then you won't be alone all the time."

"As long as it isn't someone totally creepy," I tell him. "I don't want to worry more about who's in the garden while you're at work."

"They also can't be super hot," he tells me with a grin. "Don't worry, Amy. I'm on it. I'll take care of everything, and you won't have to be scared in our house ever again."

Even though I know that that's not a promise he can really make, I believe him.

That's on me.

8

TIM

Two o'clock the next afternoon rolls around, and I actually feel nervous, like I'm about to go on a date or something. I handle HR problems at work all the time, but I'm generally on the firing end of working with people. Hiring someone, especially someone who will be living on my property, is another thing entirely.

But if I thought I was nervous, it's nothing compared to how Amy is acting. She's changed her outfit three times already, like she's going on a date with the man, and is now making a pot of tea that we can all share outside on the porch.

"Do you think I should also make lemonade?" she calls from the kitchen into the living room, where I'm sitting on the sofa, trying to scroll through the news on my phone.

"Do I what?" I call back, glancing once behind me out the window to look out for Paul. He's supposed to be here anytime now, but I know the directions to our house can be a little tricky. Holly assured me she'd make sure he could find the place and not to worry, but every second that ticks on the wall clock across from me makes me wonder if she was right.

"Should I also make lemonade?" Amy appears in the door, holding up a pitcher, her head cocked to the side. "I want to make a good first impression on Paul, and the last thing I want is to assume that he's a tea drinker and for him to wonder why we're crazy enough to offer him a hot beverage when it's not super chilly out."

Leaving my phone on the sofa, I cross the room to Amy. "I think you're overthinking this," I tell her, giving her a kiss. "I think we're going to meet this man, he's going to be great, like Holly promised, and then we're going to hire him. No big deal."

"No big deal," she repeats; then we hear the sound of a car door slamming in the driveway. "I'll get the tea!" She scurries away from me.

I plaster a huge smile on my face before going out to the front porch.

In truth, I'm glad Amy's as nervous as I am. I trust Holly and believe she would have found the best person for the job, but it's still a little unnerving to invite someone to live on your property, especially when you don't really know them. I guess this afternoon is our chance to get to know him, but I'm still nervous.

As soon as I see Paul walk from the driveway up the path to the house, though, all my nerves disappear. He's older than I imagined, around my dad's age, with some gray hair around his temples and a shiny bald spot on top. I know it's terrible, but seeing his thinning hair and how he walks with a bit of a stoop, I'm glad I won't have to worry about Amy having eye candy to look at all day long when I'm at work.

"Paul," I say, giving him a grin and holding out my hand to shake his when he reaches the porch. "I'm Tim."

He grips my hand tight, much stronger than I would have thought he was just looking at him, then gestures at the property behind me. "Gorgeous place you have here, Tim. Thanks for having me out to talk."

"Thank you. Amy, that's my wife, and I thought we could handle it all on our own, but it's getting a bit too much. Then we saw the caretaker's cottage down through the garden and thought that hiring someone to live here might take care of all our problems."

"That would be the plan," he tells me, then follows my lead and sits in a rocking chair. "You two been here long?"

"Just a week," Amy says, pushing open the screen door with her hip to join us outside. She's carrying a tray with a teapot, three cups, an assortment of tea bags, and a plate of cookies. This she sets down in front of us and then sits next to me. "It's a bit daunting," she admits, then picks up the pot. "Tea?"

"Please." Paul stares at her as she pours the water, then chooses a tea bag, putting it in his mug before turning his attention back to the gardens. "Tell me what vision you have for the place."

"Well," I say, clearing my throat, "I don't know if Holly told you, but right now we're looking at a one-month trial run to see it this is the right fit for us."

He nods.

I relax a little before continuing, "Great. So I'm not sure if everything we want done could be accomplished in a month, but we want the entire place cleaned up, the ivy taken off the house and any repairs made, the gardens cleared and prepared for spring."

"The koi pond needs some work done, and then we'd like it to be functional," Amy says, leaning forward so that she's in the conversation. "And there are walking paths through the woods, but they're all grown over, and some of the bricks in the paths are missing. We would love to have those taken care of, too."

"You two are definitely looking at a year-round caretaker with all of that," Paul says, speaking more to my wife than to me. "But there's no reason why someone couldn't make a pretty good dent in the to-do list in a month. I have a good feeling that after just a month, you'll be begging them to stay on. I'd probably start with the gardens so you could have a holiday party if you wanted to, and not have to worry about your guests tripping over everything. The ivy on the house is a concern, but waiting a few months to tackle it isn't going to make a big difference."

When I glance at Amy, I see her staring at him, a huge smile on her face. This is what we needed, just a little help to get the house and gardens under control; then our lives here will be perfect.

Paul stands and looks out over the gardens. "Those fruit trees back there need to be pruned way back, or you're not going to get anything from them."

"We have fruit trees?" Amy sounds excited and stands up to look. "Where? What kind?"

"Back along the edge of the garden," Paul says, pointing. When she nods to confirm she's seen them, he continues, "Though it's impossible to tell from here, I'd wager you have some apple and pear. Maybe fig if you're lucky."

"How in the world do you know all that? That's incredible." Amy grins at him and then elbows me gently in the ribs. "I'd love to hear what else you see here and what you think we could do."

I immediately pick up on Amy's hint. She's on board with this guy, and I need to lock it down. If he changes his mind now and walks out, I can only imagine how upset she'd be. "Would you like to see the cottage? It's really great, and you'd be welcome to live there of course, in addition to getting a paycheck each week."

Paul grins. "Lead the way. You two seem lovely. You know,

I told Holly I wasn't sure if I wanted to be a caretaker again after so many years of being out of the game, but she promised me you two were wonderful and I'd really enjoy working here. I'm beginning to think she was right, especially if you keep baking." Taking a cookie, he winks at Amy.

I don't feel the least bit jealous. He's not hitting on her. He's just being friendly, and I really like the man.

"Well, let's get moving." Feeling more and more excited about how Paul could transform our property into something even more beautiful, I lead the way down the stairs and path to the garden. "Just keep an eye out for briars," I warn him. "Amy got snagged pretty badly yesterday, and we had to bandage her leg up."

He clicks his tongue. "That's no good. It's why I'm here, Tim. Bring me on board, and I'll help protect you and your wife, I guarantee it."

I hadn't yet mentioned anything about this arrangement making Amy feel safer when she's at home by herself, but I love what he just said. Before he leaves today I'm going to talk to him about my trip to Raleigh coming up just to give him a heads-up that Amy will be alone. Paul seems like a great guy, and I should know. I've always been told I'm an incredible judge of character.

9

AMY

"We have a caretaker!" I feel silly, but I spray the whipped cream on our coffees before bringing them to the breakfast table. After hiring Paul yesterday, we took the rest of the afternoon off from gardening, which was a lovely way to spend Sunday before starting work again today.

I'm not only excited to have breakfast with Tim, but also that Paul starts today.

I know Tim has to get a move on soon so that he's not late for work, but I really wanted to celebrate a little bit with him. Whipped cream on our coffee is a far cry from popping open a bottle of champagne, but Paul stayed for a while yesterday afternoon, talking and touring the property, and by the time he left, I was too tired to even consider alcohol.

"We have a caretaker," Tim repeats, clinking his mug against mine. "For a month, remember. Then if we like him, we can talk about hiring him full time."

"I like him," I announce, sitting down to my bowl of oatmeal. It might not be the most exciting meal I could make, but it'll keep me full until it's time to wander away from my computer for lunch. "And he's so smart! How does he know so much about our property? He seemed to know a lot when we were walking around."

"I think he's just that good." He swipes his finger through the whipped cream on his coffee and licks it off, making me laugh. "Besides, when you've been doing this sort of thing for as long as he has, it makes sense he'd have an idea for how the gardens would be laid out and what kind of trees would be planted where. It's kinda like how you're so good at your job and I'm so good at mine."

"That's fair." I'm hungrier than I thought I would be, and I eat quickly before glancing at the time. "Didn't you say you have to head in early this morning?"

"Crap, yeah. Marie wanted me to come in and look over some applications for the new staff that will be working under me. I'll try to be home for dinner, Amy, but I might be late. Let me know how things go with Paul, okay? I love you."

"Love you," I say as he drops a kiss on the top of my head. Then, just like that, he's out the door, and I'm all alone again. I'm getting used to all the time I spend by myself, but I still wish he were around a bit more. Still, his job more than pays for all our expenses, and that means I can spend as much time writing as I like.

Now that Paul is going to be puttering around outside, I won't feel like I'm all alone. He'll be able to keep an eye out for anything weird, like someone walking in the gardens or moving a teacup around. I haven't told Tim, because I know he'd just get upset, but I still don't think he was the one who moved the little teacup.

It just makes no sense, but then again, any alternative I can come up with makes even less sense. What, do I honestly believe someone came into the house to put a teacup in our cupboard while we were working outside on the briars?

No, I don't. Because that's insane.

Still, after cleaning up the kitchen, I make sure to double-check all the doors are locked. Holly assured us we're the only ones with keys, but I still want to talk to Tim about having someone out to change all the locks. Call it peace of mind.

I'm about to head up the stairs to start working when someone knocks on the door. Turning, I glance down from my spot on the stairs to try to see who's there, but the small windows on either side of the huge wooden door aren't positioned correctly for me to see anyone.

It has to be Paul, though, and I'm actually excited to say hi to him this morning. Anything is better than locking myself up in my office and working for clients. I'd much rather be working on my book, but that's not top of the to-do list this morning. To be honest, I really like the man, and I can't wait to see what sort of magic he's going to be able to work on the property.

Sure enough, when I swing the door open, Paul's on my front porch, a bouquet of flowers in his hand. "I brought these for you this morning, Amy," he tells me, "as a thank-you for the job and a promise of what you're going to enjoy in the spring. I know I'm just here for a month unless something changes, but I really think you have a beautiful home, and I can't wait to see what it looks like in all its glory."

"You didn't need to do that," I say, happily taking the flowers from him anyway. "Seriously, thank you."

Am I supposed to invite him in now? I'm not sure what the etiquette is here, but before I can worry about it, he inclines his head and takes a step back.

"I have some moving in to do, and then I'm going to start working in the garden. If I need anything—"

"You just come bang on the door, and I'll either get it for you, or we'll figure it out. If we don't have what you need, feel free to buy it, and we'll pay you back." That was what Tim and I had decided to offer after my husband pointed out it wasn't fair to ask Paul to buy his own tools and equipment.

A huge grin spreads across his face. "Sounds perfect, Amy. Thank you. I have a feeling we're going to get along just great."

"I agree." I really need to get started on my writing this morning, but I don't want to be rude and shut the door in his face. Luckily for me, he inclines his head and steps back again.

"I'll try not to bother you, but maybe tonight you'd like to come see what I've gotten done. Happy writing, Amy."

"Thanks," I tell him, shutting the door and locking it. I wince as I slide the dead bolt into place. Will he have heard it and wonder why I want to make sure he's completely locked out? I guess I can't worry about being rude, but I don't want to hurt his feelings.

Humming to myself, I carry the flowers into the kitchen to put them in a vase. They're going to go right on my desk upstairs so I can enjoy them while I'm writing. It isn't until I'm seated behind my computer and looking out the window that I realize he knew I was a writer even though I don't think we'd told him that.

Maybe Tim did, yesterday, when I wasn't paying attention. Or maybe Holly told him, because I'm sure she knows what Tim and I both do for work. I'm not going to worry about it, because I have a feeling that after a month of all three of us living so close together, we're going to know an awful lot more about each other.

Paul had a slim gold band on his finger, but I didn't want to ask him about his wife. She must be a pretty special woman to be okay with him moving out for a month to fix up our property. I'll definitely have to find out more about her later as we get to know each other better, just because I'm super nosy.

Tim always says it's one of my worst traits, but I can't help it. I just like knowing things about people. That thought in mind, I fire up my computer and do a quick search for caretakers named Paul in our area.

Nothing. Not a single hit, although it's not like I really expected to learn all his deepest and darkest secrets from a simple online search. Sighing, I minimize the browser window and glance outside once more before opening my Word doc.

Watching Paul work sounds a lot more interesting than actually putting words down for my latest client, but he's probably moving into the cottage right now. It might be a while before anything really exciting starts happening in the garden, but then I'm going to be sure to take some breaks to see what he's doing.

It's so weird to think a stranger could change your life, but that's exactly what Paul is going to do, especially if we get to keep him on year-round.

10

PAUL

*S*he reminds me so much of Wilma.

I almost gawked yesterday when I saw Amy for the first time. She's young, like Wilma was when we first met, with bright eyes that locked onto me when she greeted me and a smile that reaches her eyes when she's really happy.

I feel like I'm losing my mind, and I pause on the porch for a moment, trying to gather my thoughts. She and Tim are here for a reason, and I'm here for a reason, and I can't lose sight of that. I have to punish Tim for what he did to Wilma, what he did to our family.

I'm supposed to drive Amy insane and then kill her. *That's the plan.* That's my end goal. The thought of reaching my goal is the only thing that's kept me going this long.

Holly didn't tell me that Amy looks like Wilma when she told me about the two of them. But how would she have known that looking at Amy would make my breath catch in my throat?

Amy's back in the house, and I force myself off the porch to go stand in the garden. There I take a deep breath, allowing the fresh air to fill my lungs. It's been a long time since anyone has lived in this house and even longer since the gardens have been in great condition. Turning, I eyeball the house and am disappointed at the state it's in. Even though I've been living in the cottage, I haven't had the energy to work on the garden.

I've wanted to sleep, to mourn Wilma. The last thing I wanted was to work in the garden.

Her garden.

I've been living in the cottage and avoiding the main house, where I would miss Wilma. There wasn't any way I could keep everything in working order in the main house, or clean up the garden; the memories of Wilma are too strong.

I can fix it, of course. I can fix everything. That's why Tim and Amy hired me, and I'm going to do everything I can to bring this house back to its former glory. They were so surprised yesterday when they realized I knew so much about the property and the different plants and trees here. It was easy to tell them I knew it all just because I'm that good at plant ID and that experienced when working in gardens, but that wasn't the entire truth.

The real truth is that I'm that good at identifying plants and trees in their garden because I've seen this place in its full glory. I know what it looks like in the spring when the apple and pear trees are in bloom and the way their spent petals fall like snowflakes to the ground. I know how great the little pond can look when it's all cleaned out and how smooth the path underfoot can be when the bricks aren't disrupted by roots and weeds.

I know everything there is to know about the garden, but that's not all.

I also know everything there is to know about the house.

I heard how Amy slid the dead bolt shut after I gave her the flowers, but honestly, I'd expect nothing less from her. I don't blame her for wanting to be careful and doing everything she can to keep herself safe in that big house when Tim is off working. She doesn't know me, so of course she wants to lock all her doors.

She has no way of knowing I'm here to hurt her, but she's obviously spooked enough to want to lock herself in the house.

She doesn't know I'm the one who moved the teacup into her kitchen cupboard. She has no idea she interrupted me about to drink a nice cup of tea in the cottage that day when she was supposed to be in the house. I was as surprised as she was when she came down to the cottage, but those little surprises can't keep happening.

It makes sense they would reach out to Holly to help them find a caretaker. She'd promised me she'd planted the seed in Tim's mind about hiring someone to help, and it had worked. I never should have doubted her. Still, having them come to me for my help was a much better idea than the one that I had, which was to go up to the house and offer them help out of the blue.

There would have been too many questions if I'd done that. I might have had to come clean about knowing the property just to get an interview, but Holly was right. She primed them for the idea of hiring help, and they came running as soon as things got hard.

Shaking my head, I look around the garden. The amount of work that needs to be done here is astronomical. There's no way the two of them could tackle it on their own, work their real day jobs, and still have a good relationship. No, they need someone who knows the land and who isn't afraid to put in the long hours.

I love this land, and I'm going to be the one to bring it back to its former glory. When all is said and done, it'll be mine.

Again.

Rubbing my hands together, I walk to my car and grab my duffel bag from the back seat. The cottage is all ready for someone to move in to, but that's just because I've been living there off and on for so long already. It won't take me ten minutes to pretend I'm unpacking and moving in, but I know Amy has her computer at the window that looks right over the garden and my cottage, so I need to make it look like I'm a little busy.

There's a book I've been meaning to read, and I'll get through a few chapters before finally coming out to start working. That will make her think I took my time moving in and getting settled.

I hurry down the path, moving deftly around the plants that need to be cut back, then let myself into the cottage. It feels like home because it is home, and in just a few minutes I have everything unpacked. This duffel was the one I crammed full of all my clothes and toiletries when Holly told me the house was selling.

I'd been able to grab it and leave quickly when Amy spooked me that day down here. Of course, Holly let me crash on her couch until she was able to make sure Tim and Amy were going to hire me.

After all, what else are daughters for?

11

TIM

I've been going to work so early and getting home so late that I still haven't seen Paul at work in the garden. Amy promises me he's been out there working hard every single day, so when I finally get off work at a decent hour on Thursday, I speed home and throw on some jeans and work boots so my wife and I can go check out all his hard work.

After all, I'm paying him good money to be here for the month, so I want to make sure things are actually getting done. It's hard for me to pay someone and not check up on what they're doing, even though Amy assures me that everything is fine.

She isn't in the house when I get home, so I head out into the garden to look for her. Immediately, I can see the work Paul has done, and there's a huge difference. The path is actually clear, and I can walk down it without worrying about tripping or having my leg snagged by some thorns.

There's a large pile of branches by the fruit trees that look like they're destined to become a bonfire, and I feel excitement shoot through my body. Maybe, if we hold off on burning them for a month or so, we can have some friends over and host a dinner party and bonfire. It would be really fun not only to see everyone, but to show off our house.

"Amy?" I call as I walk through the garden. "Are you out here?"

"By the koi pond!" She sounds excited.

I turn off the main path, picking my way through some taller weeds Paul hasn't gotten round to yet.

When I reach her, she's crouched by the edge of the pond, watching Paul. He has his waders on and is in the murky rainwater that's half-filled the pond, a huge stick in one hand, his other gripping something tightly in his palm.

"What are you two doing?" I ask, sitting down next to my wife to watch.

"Paul found some money people have thrown in the pond," she says excitedly. "He invited me out to see what else was in here."

"That's cool." Now I'm interested, not because I think there will be anything really valuable in the pond, but because my wife is so excited. Who knows, maybe there will be some relics from the people who owned the house before us.

Paul waves and makes his way over to us, holding out his hand for me to take what's in it.

When I reach out, he drops a coin into my palm. I poke at it, wiping some of the sludge from it onto my jeans.

"Looks like there were kids who lived here before and dropped stuff in the pond," Paul says. "That, or people used to come up here on the property and roam around and toss stuff in. You guys had any issues with strangers on the property?"

I glance at Amy, who raises an eyebrow at me. I don't want to embarrass her in front of Paul, and I'm surprised at the information she volunteers.

"Actually, I think someone was living in the cottage before

you moved in," she says, picking at a seam on her shirt. "I went down to the cottage, and there was a teacup there with hot tea in it. When I called the police and we went down there a bit later, it was gone, so I don't know if I imagined it or if someone was really there."

"That's scary stuff." Paul leans on his stick and looks at my wife, compassion written all over his face. "I imagine you were pretty upset."

"Yeah, and that's one of the reasons why I'm so glad that you're here now. Nobody is going to be hiding down in the cottage if you live there."

"You don't have to worry about that now," he agrees, giving her a nod before glancing over at me. "It's been fun, Amy, but now that Tim is home, I bet you two have something you'd rather do than watch me play in the muck. I'll bring whatever else I find up to the house, how does that sound?"

"Sounds great," I say before Amy can respond. "Amy, why don't we head on up to the house? I feel like I haven't seen you in forever."

My wife stands, brushing off the seat of her pants, but I get the feeling she would rather stay and find out what else Paul is going to pull from the pond. A flash of irritation shoots through me, but I push it away. It's not her fault that it's actually fun to see what might be hiding in the murky water, but I miss my wife.

"Thanks for letting me watch, Paul," she says, then joins me on the path. "Can't wait to see what else you find."

He raises his hand in response.

Amy and I hurry back to the house. Once inside, I pour us each a glass of wine and hand her one.

"Something's up," she says, tilting her head to look at me. "What's the wine for?"

"I just missed you today," I tell her. "And Marie gave me the dates for my first leadership class."

That gets her attention, like I was sure it would. She takes a sip of her wine and raises an eyebrow to encourage me to continue.

"I'll be going to Raleigh next week."

"North Carolina?" She puts her wine down on the counter and crosses her arms. "Why do you have to go there? Isn't there something here in Tennessee?"

"I asked the same thing, but Marie told me this is the best class." I don't want to tell Amy that when I'd seemed a little bit on the fence about going all the way to Raleigh, Marie mentioned she might be able to find someone else to do the job. I've always known my boss was cutthroat, but that seemed a little harsh.

"Okay. Please tell me it's just one week."

"Not even," I assure her. "It's really just a few days, at least for now, but there will be more. No big deal, okay? I promise it'll be fine, especially with you and Paul getting along so well. He'll be around to make sure no one else is on the property."

"You're right." She smiles at me, but I can tell that she's just putting on a brave face. "Oh, I meant to ask you this morning, did you see my perfume when you were getting ready? I can't find it, and I don't think I would have just misplaced it."

"Nope," I tell her. "Sorry to say, but I'm not in the habit of wearing my wife's perfume to the office."

She laughs and smacks my shoulder, and I'm relieved that she no longer seems upset about me leaving for a week. We both knew this was going to happen and that it was part of the deal for me getting the raise, but I really hoped that I wouldn't get any pushback from Amy about it.

"Well, I must have been on autopilot the other morning

and put it somewhere I don't normally. I'm sure it'll turn up." She shrugs and takes another sip of her wine. "What do you want for dinner?"

"Lasagna," I say, knowing full well there's one in the freezer. "You?"

"You read my mind, dear husband." Laughing, she crosses the kitchen to the freezer and pulls it out before checking the box and preheating the oven.

I watch as she gets some plates and glasses out, and then turn my attention out the kitchen window. I wish we could see more of the property from here, but until more of the weeds are knocked down, the best view is from the second floor or attic. Still, I see a flash of movement in the garden, and I'm sure it's Paul walking back from the koi pond.

"I'm going to go see if Paul found anything else in the pond," I tell Amy before hurrying out of the kitchen. It takes me a moment to pull my boots back on and walk down the path to where the path to the koi pond splits off, but I don't see him.

Strange. I would have sworn I saw him here. He was whistling a moment ago, but now I can't hear him.

Turning away from the koi pond, I notice some of the weeds and other plants have been trampled down a little bit. Perhaps he came this way, and I just missed him. He did say he would bring anything else that he found up to the house for us to see, but he was probably being polite and didn't want to interrupt our evening.

He seems thoughtful like that. I don't want to bother him, but I am really curious about what else he found. With my luck, he'll bring it to the house tomorrow to show us, and I'll be at work. I don't want to miss it, so I turn away from the koi pond and follow the pressed-down grasses.

I haven't walked this way around the garden yet. Passing the fruit trees, I come to a low stone wall that's half crumbling. I'm sure Paul will take care of it if we keep him on full time, and I clamber over it, being careful not to knock any more stones loose. From here the yard seems to fall away, a sloping hill that leads right down to the woods.

I don't see him.

He was here, I swear it. Either him or someone else was walking through the garden, but there's no way I'm going to tell Amy I saw someone who might not be Paul.

Somehow I missed him, or he disappeared. Turning slowly in a circle, I look for where he could have gone. He was wearing a bright red shirt, so he should be easy to spot, but it's like he passed through a hidden door and walked out of the garden, and I have no idea where he could have gone.

12

PAUL

Hurrying through the door to the basement, I turn and quickly shut it, making sure to lean against it so I can lock it from the inside. Thick vines and weeds press up against the outside of the door, making it almost impossible to see from the outside unless you know exactly where to look.

I know, of course, because I've passed through this door hundreds of times. It leads to one of my favorite places in the house, and that's where I'm going now, my bag full of treasures I pulled out of the koi pond.

I gave Tim that silly little coin I found because I knew it would make him happy, but I never imagined he would come out of the house and come looking for me again. It was foolish of me to tell them that I'd bring what I found up to the house for them to see because now he wants to know if I have any treasures to share.

I don't. Not with him, anyway.

Switching on the flashlight I keep in my pocket, I hurry down the corridor until it opens up into a small room. There's a wooden door I can shut to keep the room completely safe from prying eyes, but I don't see a reason to close and lock it yet. It's not like Amy and Tim have done a lot of exploring on the property.

Inside, I put my bag down on the table and begin to empty it. Most of the things I found in the pond aren't worth anything, and these are what I'll take to the new owners of the house, but there are a few things here I remember throwing into the water when I was younger.

There's some jewelry I stole from my aunt and threw into the water to punish her. A handful of dirty coins are still a little wet when I put them on the table. There's spoons and forks that I threw in there to punish my mom, and a few of them are silver. I keep the silver ones out and put the plain ones back in the bag to take to Amy and Tim.

If I thought they would stay out of my cottage, I'd keep all my finds there, but Amy is nosy. I could tell that right off when I met her. It was obvious she was dying to ask me about the wedding ring I wear, but that's not information I'm willing to offer up without something in return.

Turning to the shelf by the door, I pick up her bottle of perfume and spritz it in the air. It smells delicious, light and airy, and I waft it through the room to really enjoy the scent.

As much as I'd like to stay down here and take pleasure in what I'm collecting, it's been a long day in the sun, and I'm ready for bed.

Before I go, though, I turn to the little shrine I made for Wilma. There are a few candles I like to burn when I'm down here for a while, as well as her wedding ring, her favorite necklace, and a photo of her. It's all set up just the way I like it, with her favorite perfume right next to her photo.

Hesitating, I pick up the perfume and heft the little bottle in my hand. I'm still holding Amy's in the other, and I pause for a moment, unsure of what I'm about to do.

Then I put Amy's perfume down in place of Wilma's. It

feels strange to do, but I don't think Wilma would mind. Turning, I put Wilma's perfume on the shelf by the door.

There. That's good. I have my space to remember Wilma, but it's okay to have something of Amy's there too. They're so alike.

I'm a little regretful when I close the door and lock it behind me after shouldering my bag. It's a quick walk down the hall, but I don't want to go outside just yet.

I want to see what Tim and Amy are doing. Mostly Amy, if I'm honest. I want to get one last look at her before I go down to the cottage for the night. Tim came outside looking for me, and the last thing I want is for him to see me coming out of my secret door, so instead of going outside, I detour to a small ladder that leads up into the ceiling.

Here's the thing about old houses like this that a lot of people don't know—there's a lot of extra space that most people can't account for. Space runs behind the walls, making it easy for someone to move through the house if they know what they're doing and where they're going. There are hidden doors in the house, as well as ones that are not quite so hidden, like the one in the foyer.

I watched Amy from there the first day. She felt my eyes on her, I'm sure of it, but I keep the hinges well oiled so they don't make a sound when I open or close them. The last thing I want is for anyone to know I'm moving through the small passages built into the walls.

At the ceiling I pause, one hand on the ladder, then reach up and push the trapdoor open. It swings up, and I grab the leather strap attached to it to lower it silently so I can climb through. My heart pounds hard as I listen for the sound of footsteps. Usually I can figure out exactly where Amy and Tim are just by listening for a moment before I venture into the walls.

What they don't know is there are a number of secret

passages built into the home. The door in the foyer is just the entrance to one of many, and it's not even the one I like to use the most.

The sound of banging attracts my attention, and I push through a small door that leads into the living room. It opens right behind where my parents had a piano when I was growing up, and I crawl through it. When the door is shut, it blends in perfectly with the paneling that's on all the walls in the room, but I leave it propped open right now so I can get back through it quickly.

"I think we need him full time," Amy says, her voice carrying to me from the kitchen.

I can't see her, but when I close my eyes, I can practically picture her in there. She'll probably have on an apron, which I've seen her wear before, and most definitely will have a glass of wine in her hand.

"He's great. Have you seen the work he's done on the roses so far?"

"I thought you weren't supposed to trim roses back until the spring," Tim says.

I narrow my eyes even though he can't see me.

"Sure, because you know so much about that." Amy laughs. "But seriously, Tim, it's nice to have him here when you're at work. I can't always see him working, of course, but I know he's there, and that makes me feel safe."

"Good. That's what I want."

I make her feel safe.

There's the clatter of dishes and silverware, and I freeze, worried that they might come into the dining room to eat, but so far it seems they like to eat at the small table they have set up in the kitchen. The dining room table is covered with boxes anyway, all of them still waiting to be unpacked.

"It's just weird, isn't it, about my perfume? I swear I put it down in the same place I always do."

"You told me yourself you were really stressed out about the move and trying to juggle so many clients," Tim points out. "I bet you anything we'll go up there after dinner and it'll be right where you left it, probably under the sink by the cleaning supplies or something."

It won't be. I didn't spray the perfume directly on myself, but when I take a deep breath, I can smell it anyway. It thrills me to think that I'm wearing Amy's perfume, and she has no idea I took it, but I do feel a pang of regret that she's missing it. I wanted to scare her at first, wanted her to feel like she was losing her mind.

Now I feel a strange pang of guilt over that too, but I push it away.

"You're probably right. So do you leave Sunday, or when?" Amy's voice is almost drowned out by the sound of her opening the oven door. It squeaks loudly, and I wince, wanting nothing more than to get some WD-40 to spray on it. Even though it was hard to make out her words, I'm sure I heard her correctly.

"Yeah, Sunday. And I won't be back until late Friday night sometime. I don't know for sure what time the last class gets over on Friday, but I have a good feeling I won't be on the road until after lunch."

"How long is the drive?"

"Seven hours, give or take with traffic. I'll let you know when I'm on the way, of course, but if I hit rush hour around Knoxville, then I'll be delayed. Do you want me to tell Paul I'll be gone so he can keep a close eye on the property and you?"

I lean forward, wanting to be nearer to Amy when she replies. Honestly, I can't wait to hear what she's going to say. Does she want me to know? Does she want me to look out for her?

"No, you don't have to. I might tell him eventually, but

we're not there yet, not that close. I don't want him to feel like he has to stop everything to watch me."

I'm disappointed, but it doesn't matter. Amy doesn't want to bother me, which is nice of her.

But I'm still going to keep an eye on her. She'll just never know.

13

AMY

I have to admit that even though I'm a little worried about rambling around in our new house all by myself, I'm also really excited to have some time alone. I love my husband, this isn't about that, but there's nothing like staying up late eating ice cream and binge-watching terrible eighties movies without him making snide remarks about the acting or wanting to go to bed early.

So after he left last night, I moped around the house for what I thought was an appropriate amount of time, then called the Chinese place twenty minutes away. I put in an order that would be more than enough for three people, which means I'll have leftovers for days, and queued up some terribly trashy TV.

Working from home isn't always easy but should come with some perks, which is why I wanted to stay up late and sleep in this morning. By the time I finally get up, the sun is shining right through my curtains, and I can hear Paul whistling outside while he works.

At first, his constant whistling was a bit unnerving. He

does it all the time, no matter if he's weeding or leaning on his shovel, taking a break from digging up plants to transplant them. The sound is constant, but it's becoming something I'm getting used to, like the background ticking of a clock.

With my bedroom window open so I can catch the cool night breeze before it warms up, I can hear him whistling like he's right in the room with me. Wrapping a robe around myself, I go to the window and look down into the yard to try to spot him. He likes wearing bright T-shirts, I've noticed, and sometimes has on a tan hat, so he's fairly easy to spot, but I can't see him.

"He's always happy in the morning," I say to myself as the whistling fades. He's probably around the side of the house now where I can't see him. Rather than wondering about him, I need to shower and get something to eat so I can start working.

In the bathroom I shower quickly and dress before heading downstairs. It's weird to make breakfast for myself and not for Tim, so I pull out some bacon I'd kept hiding in the back of the fridge so Tim doesn't eat it all, and whip up my own version of a bacon, egg, and cheese sandwich.

Twenty minutes later I'm sitting outside on the front porch, watching the clouds sweep by and wondering how much writing I'm going to get done today. It's not that I don't love writing. It's just that after sleeping in this morning and having a lazy breakfast, I'm feeling a bit ... uninspired, shall we say. I'd much rather work on the book I'm writing than write blogs for my copywriting clients.

"You have to get your butt in gear, Amy," I tell myself, then leave my plate out on the porch, grab my sneakers from by the door, and pull them on. A nice walk around the property is sure to wake me up and get my blood pumping. Then I won't feel so sluggish when I do finally sit down to write, and maybe I'll have a bit more inspiration.

I don't even realize I'm heading in the direction of the cottage until I'm halfway down the path through the garden. It's so nice to actually walk along this path without tripping over anything. Paul has done a great job not just cutting back the various plants that were growing too close to the path, but also removing the moss and dirt that had accumulated over the stone path.

I can see it for the first time since we moved in, and I'm beginning to get an idea of how gorgeous this property will be when it's all said and done.

Whistling from across the line of fruit trees draws my attention, and I see Paul for the first time today. He's too far away for me to have to speak, but I don't want him to see me and think I'm being rude, so I turn from the main path he's been working on and cut across some of the more overgrown parts of the garden. When I finally get to him, he's gathering up the branches he pruned from the fruit trees last week and dragging them into the middle of the garden to stack them in a pile.

"Good morning," I call as I walk up behind him. I don't know exactly how old he is, but the last thing I want is to scare him and give him a heart attack.

"Oh, Amy," he says, dropping his stack of branches and turning to look at me. "How are you this morning?"

"Great." I point at the pile. "You planning on having a bonfire or something?"

"I was going to ask Tim if he wanted to do that or if he wanted me to take care of it. Looks like there's going to be some bad weather later this week, so I wanted to get the branches burned before they got soaked."

I had no idea the weather was going to turn nasty. "I think

he'd probably really appreciate it if you did it yourself," I tell him. "He's actually gone through the end of the week."

"Gone?" Paul sounds genuinely surprised, which means he probably didn't notice that Tim left last night. If he had, he might have wondered where my husband was going and why he hadn't returned. "Where did he go without you?"

"Work stuff," I tell him, shrugging. "It's no big deal, though. I like being on my own, and I have no doubt I'm going to get a lot of writing done."

"Oh, he did mention that." Paul smiles at me, and I can't help but smile back. "I've just been enjoying myself out here and didn't remember when he was leaving. Do you want to help me with the bonfire? We could do it tonight." He looks excited at the prospect of the two of us having a fire together.

I hesitate, not because I don't want to have a bonfire out here in the garden under a clear sky where we can see all the stars, but because I just don't know Paul that well. I'm sure Tim wouldn't mind if I joined him, right? Paul's got to be as old as my parents, so it's not like anything would ever happen.

"I think that sounds great," I tell him, deciding I'll agree to the bonfire without checking in with Tim. What is there to check in on, anyway? It's not like Paul and I are going on vacation together. He's the caretaker, for goodness' sake. "And I'll make dinner, how does that sound?" I'm actually a little excited about the idea of making him dinner. I love to cook, and it's always fun to cook for new people.

"I think that sounds perfect," he tells me, with an easy grin.

I feel myself relax. There's something really calming about Paul. I have a pretty good feeling very few things could ever rile or upset him.

He turns away from me and continues stacking the cut branches. Even though I know I should let him get on with work and go write myself, I don't want to go inside. The thought of sitting at my computer all day when the weather is so gorgeous is enough to make me feel sick, but if I don't get my article turned in soon, I'm not going to have a job for much longer.

It's not that my writing brings in a ton of income when compared to what Tim makes, but I really love contributing to our little family. Once we start having kids, I'm not sure if I'll be able to find the time to write, but I'm going to try. The last thing I want is for Tim to feel like he has to make all the money we need.

"Everything okay?" Paul looks at me, kindness in his eyes.

"Oh, it's great," I tell him, throwing a smile on my face. "Really. I'd just rather be out here in the sun and wind than inside at my computer, that's all."

"Feel free to walk around as much as you want, it's your property, but I have to warn you that some of the paths I haven't cleared yet look a little dangerous."

"Dangerous?" Without thinking, I turn around and look in the direction I came from.

"Not so much that one," he tells me, and I glance back at him. "But some of them have poison oak and ivy on them, and some are also covered with loose rocks. The last thing I want is for you to trip and sprain your ankle or something. Best to stick to the ones I've cleared."

"Thank you." I'm scanning the ground now, looking for the poison ivy and oak he was talking about, but I don't know them from any other creeping vine that has taken over the property. "I guess I'll leave you to it, then. But I will be back down for dinner."

"I'll make sure you have a nice safe path to walk on," Paul promises me. "The last thing I want is for anything to happen to you, especially while Tim is away. Don't you worry, Amy, I'll look out for you."

He's looking out for me.

I don't know why that makes me feel so good. It probably has something to do with my dad not being around much when I was a little kid, but I really appreciate what Paul just said. He's going to look out for me, and I'm going to have a great week while Tim is away.

14

PAUL

I watch Amy as she picks her way carefully back to the house. Of course there isn't any poison ivy or oak here to snag her ankles, and most of the loose rocks that might trip her are so big and obvious I can't imagine anyone not seeing them when they are out walking.

But I don't want her wandering around the property. I doubt she or Tim are aware enough of what's going on around them to find my secret entrance to the house, but I don't want to risk it. She's the one who would pay more attention, I believe, because she's curious.

It should bother me, but it doesn't, not really. Wilma always liked to know everything about everyone, too. I'm used to the women around me wanting to know what I'm up to. It's just one more thing about Amy that reminds me of Wilma.

Honestly, though, I'm a little surprised she came clean with me about Tim being gone so easily, but that tells me she's starting to trust me more. Of course, I knew he was going to be out of town this week, just like I know that she had a wonderful first night by herself. She made sure to lock all the doors to the house to stay safe and keep people out, but that didn't stop me from coming in through the walls to check on her.

She's so peaceful when she sleeps. So happy.

It's just too bad she married Tim.

Just thinking about her husband makes me scowl, and I grab a branch, angrily throwing it onto the pile. I know Amy can't see me from her office, so unless she makes an effort to find me from another window, she won't see how angry I get when I think about her husband.

Tim.

It's hard for me to speak to him without letting my real feelings for him show through. At the same time, Amy is much lovelier than I would have imagined. Sure, she's nosy, and she's definitely gullible, but I don't hate her. Quite the opposite actually, the more I get to know her. She made a huge mistake marrying Tim, but that can be forgiven.

We all make mistakes. You just have to hope that the mistakes you make don't hurt other people. Amy's mistake didn't.

Tim's did.

Tim's mistake was supposed to end up with Amy getting hurt. But I'm starting to feel bad for her.

"Asshole," I mutter, throwing more wood onto the pile. The bonfire will be huge tonight, and I would love to start burning the wood now just to bring the amount down a bit to a safer level, but I don't want Amy to see the smoke and think I'm not excited about our bonfire tonight.

I'm sure she wants to get to know me, but I already feel like I know her. She's familiar to me, calm and thoughtful, just like my Wilma. Still, I want to know more about the woman who decided to marry Tim, who decided to move to this house out in the middle of nowhere, having only seen it in pictures. She has a hold on her husband, that much is for sure.

And I can see it. Turning, I look up at the house, imagining Amy up there working. It would be so easy to hurt her while Tim is away, but when I look at her, all I see is Wilma. Thinking this makes me turn my ring on my finger. What a sweet woman she was. I wish she were still alive. If she were, I might not be the caretaker here. I probably would have been able to move on after losing my job.

But I can't. Not now. Wilma was the only person who could talk me off the ledge and stop me from doing things that maybe weren't the best idea, but she's gone now. She's gone, and the only other person who gets involved in my life is Holly.

Holly. Just thinking of my daughter reminds me that I need to call her soon to check in. We talk every night so she knows how things are going with Amy and Tim. She calls them our pep talks, as if I could ever lose focus on what we're planning.

The calls are the only way I can keep her from showing up here and taking care of matters on her own.

I remember holding Wilma's hand when she died. She'd fought the cancer so long and so hard, but in the end, it didn't matter. We lost the house, and I lost her. Honestly though, I lost her long before she died when she forgot who I was.

Everyone told me I didn't have anyone to blame and that I certainly shouldn't blame myself. But I didn't blame myself, that was the thing. I know I didn't do a single thing wrong. I would have killed for Wilma if I thought it would have kept her from dying, but that wasn't an option.

Clenching my fist hard, I stare up at the house. It's silly to try to get any revenge for what happened to my beautiful wife, but I don't care. I want to honor her memory the only way I can, and this is what my daughter wants me to do.

The very first thing Tim did when he got his new job right after graduating college was help with cutbacks. I blame his boss, Marie, for what happened, but she's untouchable. Tim's the one who handpicked the person who was going to get fired. Marie stamped the paperwork.

Tim's the one who ruined my life.

I wrote a long letter explaining why I couldn't lose my job. Why I couldn't lose my health insurance. I begged TechCorp to keep me on for just a little bit longer, just through Wilma's experimental treatments, but Tim chose my paperwork from the stack of others who were also on the chopping block, and I lost my job.

Then my insurance.

And my house so that I could pay for everything.

Then my wife.

To make matters worse, I showed up drunk after hours at TechCorp, wanting to talk to Marie. She told me it was out of her hands, that Tim had been the person to decide who lost their job. She threw the words at me like they would be enough to protect her.

It worked.

He was the person who ruined my life.

Who took my job, my wife, my home.

Our home had been in terrible disrepair long before Wilma died just because I was putting in constant overtime to try to pay for her treatment. There hadn't been any time to pick up the yard, cut back the roses, or clean the ivy from the walls of the house. She was sick for so long that by the time she died, the house already looked rough.

Four more years of sitting empty and it came to this.

I kept the cottage up because I could. I didn't want to live in the big house again, not with the memories Wilma and I had built there. And as for Holly, my daughter was happy to be involved. She had a big-time job at the hospital and a hot little condo downtown, but she didn't have her mom. She'd been desperate to get started well before I came up with the plan.

In fact, I was the one who had kept her calm and made her wait.

But I'd been watching Tim and Amy. I'd seen her impassioned posts on Facebook asking if anyone knew of a house they could afford that would be the perfect home when they had kids. I knew how much the bank had foreclosed on my house for, and Holly was thrilled to pretend to be a Realtor and reach out to Amy.

Of course she fell in love with my house.

Of course they moved in.

Of course they have no idea that I lived on this property my entire life, and I have no inclination to move now.

Tim ruined my life. And now he's on my turf.

But not for long.

15

TIM

I've called Amy three times, but each time it goes straight to her voicemail, and I'm beginning to get a little bit worried about where she might be. It's weird that she wouldn't pick up when I rang her, or at least call me back. We have a little system where one phone call can be ignored if necessary, but if the person calls back again, then that suggests there's an emergency.

I'm abusing the system a little bit right now, and I'm fully aware of that, but I want to talk to my wife. It's strange not to see her at night, and I don't like wondering what she's doing.

I'm about to call her again when my phone buzzes in my hand, and I sigh with relief as I answer it.

"There you are," I say right as she speaks.

"You called three times; are you okay? Is there an emergency?"

There's real fear in her voice, and I actually feel good about that. I want her to worry about me. Maybe that's terrible, but when she wasn't picking up my calls, I was honestly getting frustrated with her.

"Everything's fine," I tell her. "The emergency was that I really missed you and wanted to talk to you." She's silent, and I'm pretty sure she's mad I abused the system, so I continue, "And I was worried about you! I hadn't heard from you all day and was starting to wonder if everything was okay."

"I was at the store and forgot my phone. No big deal."

"I thought you had all the groceries you needed for the week. What were you getting?" I'm pacing in my small hotel room and walk over to the window to look down into the city. I know there are some people who love big buildings, but I'm not one of them. I'm much happier in our small Tennessee town than here in Raleigh, and I'm already itching to get back home.

"I'm actually making dinner tonight for Paul. Well, we're burning the branches he trimmed from the fruit trees and having a bonfire, and I said I'd make dinner."

That sounds like a lot more fun than wandering downtown until I find something that looks good. Everyone thinks that eating out is a real treat, and it is, but not when you're by yourself. I don't want to be eating alone, especially not when Amy is going to be eating with someone.

"Sounds nice," I say. "What are you making?"

"Nothing too crazy. I got everything I need to make sloppy joes and have chips and cookies. I didn't want it to be too fancy since we'll be outside under the stars."

"You sure this isn't a date? It sounds really romantic." I try to keep my voice light so I sound like I'm joking, but I'm a little bit irritated. I want to be eating dinner with my wife around a bonfire under the stars, not thinking about another man getting to do that.

She sucks her teeth at me. "You do realize he could be my dad, right? It's insane of you to even question if something is going to happen." She sounds honestly irritated.

"I know, I'm sorry. I'm just feeling left out, that's all. I wish I were there with you and not on this horrible trip."

Her voice softens. "Is it that bad?"

"Pretty boring, yeah. And it's not like I don't know most of this. Marie threw me right into the fire without any concern about whether or not I knew what I was doing. Remember my first week, she had me decide who to lay off from the company?" I shake my head just thinking about it. "It was such a terrible thing to do, to just give me some folders and then ask me to decide who was staying and who was going."

"I remember that." Amy exhales hard, and I can picture her sitting down. "You were a wreck about it."

"Sure was. And now, reading all this information and going to classes and lectures, I'm not sure I did it right, just choosing one randomly without taking the time to look into them. I had no idea, though, and there's no way to go back in time and figure it out. What's done is done, and it's not like Marie would ever let me bring it up with her. In her mind, when something is finished, it's completely over, and she doesn't look back."

"And I'm guessing you don't remember the person's name?"

"I don't." Shame washes over me. I had told myself I wouldn't forget their name. I'd promised myself I'd do whatever it took to remember it because I felt so terrible about what had happened, but then I got busy, and we got married, and their name just ... slipped away from me. "How the hell am I supposed to go through that again, Amy? I don't think I can. You know I felt terrible about it, and now Marie wants me to be in charge of that again."

"Tim, you can't beat yourself up over this, okay? I'm serious. It was a long time ago, and now you know so much more about how to choose the people to let go. You and I both know you wouldn't ever intentionally do anything to hurt someone. Marie put you in a shit situation, and I wouldn't blame you if you didn't forgive her for that. But it's done, the person is probably working somewhere else and probably has a great life. I'm sure you did your best, and I know you'll do your best again when you have to. You're a good guy, Tim, definitely one of the good ones, or I wouldn't have married you. Next time you'll know to really research the employees, and you'll feel more in control of it, okay?"

I love my wife, and I really appreciate what she's saying, but I don't know that I did do my best. I didn't know what to do, and I was so nervous about making a mistake that I didn't take time to look through the folders. Marie had told me that I had all day to choose who was going to lose their job, and that I needed to take my time picking, but I hadn't.

I'd sat in my office and just stared at the folders. It hadn't been what I thought I'd signed up for. I only went into HR because my dad had worked in it, and he told me I would get to help people. He was wrong, and when Marie came to me at five asking who was going to get the boot to save the company some money, I picked a folder at random.

And now I don't remember the person's name.

"Tim, you there?" Amy sounds worried.

I give my head a little shake to clear it. "I'm here, sorry. Just kinda fell into my own thoughts there for a moment, but I'm back."

"Tim, if you don't want to work for Marie, I'm sure you can find another job somewhere else. There's no reason you have to keep working there. You're good at what you do or you wouldn't have gotten this promotion and raise. I have no doubt you could walk into another company and get a great job."

"Not now, not when we've just bought the house and want to have kids." I appreciate Amy, but she's never had a real job with office politics. She's never had the stress of being the one to carry the health insurance for someone she loves. "I would never do anything to jeopardize us, okay? You don't have to worry about me just up and quitting one day, okay?"

"Unless I become a big-time author," she says, laughing. "Then you can do whatever you want. Or, and hear me out, we could turn this place into a bed and breakfast. What do you say?"

For a moment I actually consider it. I can just see Amy getting up early in the morning to bake muffins for breakfast and hanging sheets out on the line so that guests can admire the fresh scent when they go to bed. It's idyllic. We'd keep Paul on, that's for sure, but I could do any repairs around the house.

Then I shake my head.

"It's a great thought," I tell her. "And I appreciate it. But the benefits of my job are just so good. There's no way anyone would ever walk away from them willingly, believe me. If I quit my job and something happened to you and we couldn't pay the bills, then I don't know what I'd do. No, this is the type of job you don't quit."

"Well, I love you, no matter what you do, okay? Just don't do anything drastic without talking to me first."

"I love you. Have a great time with Paul and tell him how sorry I am I'm missing the night, okay?"

"Will do." She pauses, and I look back outside. The city is alive here, people hustling to and fro on the sidewalks. It's strange to think I'm going to be out there with them in just a few minutes. "Be safe, okay? Be smart. Please."

I know what she's saying. She's asking me not to go out with someone, not to make the same mistake I have before, but I won't. The regret of what I did eats at me every single day, and I'd never make the same mistake twice.

"You do the same. Amy, I don't know what I'd ever do without you."

She laughs like I've just told her a joke and hangs up, but I'm serious. Stories about husbands losing their wives really get to me. I can't imagine living my life without Amy.

I have no idea what I'd do.

16

AMY

I'm a little nervous carrying my tray of food down to the bonfire to meet Paul. It's silly, and I know that, but he seems like a really neat guy, and I like having him around. The night is cooling off quickly, and even though I'm sure it'll be hot by the fire, I'm already chilled, so I have on a pair of jeans and one of Tim's hoodies.

It's from the company picnic last fall and has their slogan written across the chest. I always tease Tim when he wears it because it's ugly, a deep navy-blue color with hot pink writing that makes me think that the color combo had to have been on sale, but it's incredibly warm.

If I'm going to be sitting outside eating dinner on this chilly evening, then I want to make sure I'm going to be as warm as possible, even if that means I'm a walking billboard for a while. Not that Paul will ever be swayed to leave us, I'm pretty sure. I caught glimpses of him today while I was working, and he seemed incredibly happy outside.

I can't imagine a man like him being happy in an office. I know Tim wants to keep him on for just a month as a trial run, but there's no way we're going to want to let him go in the upcoming weeks, I'm sure of it. He's making a huge difference in the way this place looks already, and there's no way Tim and I are equipped to keep it up ourselves.

I can smell the bonfire before I see it, and I use my flashlight to make sure I don't trip on my way down to meet Paul. He definitely put the fear of God in me earlier when he warned me about how bad some of the paths were. I don't think he was really trying to scare me, but I made myself a promise to keep to the paths he's cleared.

Just to be safe.

As I get closer, I see him standing by the fire. He has his hands shoved in his pockets and his head tilted back as the flames leap up above him. How did I miss this? It must be the way the land slopes that I couldn't see it from the house. It's a huge bonfire, much bigger than I thought it would be, and I hesitate a moment before walking up to it. Immediately, I wish I hadn't worn the hoodie, but I'm hoping we'll sit a bit farther back from the flames so I don't feel like I'm going to melt.

"There you are," Paul says, turning to me with a smile. I think it falters as his eyes flick to the logo on my hoodie, but I'm probably imagining things. He holds up a small pouch and shakes it at me. I hear metal inside. "I was beginning to wonder if you had a better offer for tonight, and I thought I was going to have to leave the coins from the koi pond on your porch for you."

"Not a chance." I put the tray down and take the pouch from him. "Thanks for these. I'm sure Tim will love to see them. You hungry?"

"Always. I moved two stumps back there for us to sit. It should be far enough from the fire that you don't feel like you're burning up, but if you get chilly, I can move them closer." He leads the way to a pair of stumps.

I follow him, grateful to be away from the leaping flames.

"I made sloppy joes," I say, handing him his plate and a bottle of water. "You don't strike me as a vegetarian."

His laugh is loud, and I settle onto my stump. "Never. Not even once. I agree there's something to it, some good way to help save the environment, but there's nothing like a steak." He takes a big bite of his sloppy joe and nods like he's really pleased with it. "That's good. Did you make the sauce yourself?"

I nod, feeling excited. "Sure did." What I don't tell him is that I wanted him to be impressed with the food I made, so I spent a huge chunk of the afternoon working on the sauce instead of writing, but I'll just have to get up a bit earlier tomorrow to make up for it. I really wanted dinner to be good and special and figured homemade sauce was the way to go.

"You can tell. Good spices in there."

We eat in comfortable silence for a few minutes; then I steel myself to ask him some questions. I want to know more about him, including why his wife is okay with him living on our property and working here instead of being at home with her, but before I can ask a single thing, he taps his ring and looks at me.

"You're wondering about Wilma."

I blush. "I am, I'm so sorry. How did you know?"

"Kept staring at it. No worries. If we're going to be friends, then you might as well know it all. My sweet Wilma died a few years ago, but I can't bring myself to take off my ring. It's a part of me, you see. I'd feel wrong not wearing it."

I glance down at my rings. I love my engagement ring, and I helped Tim pick out my wedding band. They're small, but they're mine, and even though he's mentioned getting something bigger and more impressive to wear a few times, I don't want it. I don't mind wearing something small. He gave it to me as a sign of how much he loves me, and the size doesn't really matter. Not to me, anyway, and I doubt it would matter to someone like Paul.

"I don't think I'd be able to take mine off either," I tell him. "I'm really sorry to hear about your wife. That had to be terrible, losing her."

He nods. "It was. Damn near did me in, if I'm being honest. I've never met another person as kind and caring as she was, although you remind me of her. She lit up the room just by walking into it, and could make me happy no matter what I'd been going through. I'll never love anyone again, not the way I loved her, and I'm not going to try."

It feels good for him to compliment me like this. "That explains why you're happy here," I venture, hoping I'm not stepping on toes. "I mean, I wondered why your wife was okay with you living here and not at home with her, but if she's gone, then it makes sense you would try to find some-place where you can be happy."

He's silent for a moment, and I mentally kick myself, sure I've crossed the line this time. I don't know the guy that well, and even though he is kind, I doubt he wants me talking about his dead wife. For the first time since we sat down to share a meal, I feel awkward and almost wish I had stayed home.

"I don't really have a home." He shrugs and glances up at the house. "Not like this, anyway, not after I lost Wilma. For a long time, I lived with my daughter off and on, but she has her own life and doesn't need me crashing on her sofa all the time. This place is gorgeous, though."

"It is." I look up at the house. It's difficult to see its outline against the dark sky, but I can see where it's blocking out some of the stars. "It really seems like the perfect place to raise a family, which is something both Tim and I want. We lived in an apartment before, which was fine, but not really where I wanted to have kids. Here we can have a dog or two and some kids, and they can all run around outside."

"Seems like a perfect place to grow up," Paul agrees, and I feel myself relax. "Amy, you don't need to worry, okay? You didn't upset me talking about Wilma. I know that she's gone, but she still lives in me. Missing her makes me see just how important it is for people to love each other. You and Tim have something special, I can tell."

I wasn't sure what it would be like to have dinner with someone I don't know. No, I don't feel nervous around him, and I don't think he would do anything to hurt or scare me, but I'm still very aware of the dangers that come from spending time with men you don't know.

I would never cheat on Tim. I know how painful that is. But I also know how it might look to someone if they knew Paul and I were having dinner together without Tim.

But Paul seems different. He's just an older guy who lost his wife and is doing his best to live out the rest of his life. I can't imagine what it would be like to lose Tim and then try to survive without him around. Sure, I'm happy to be flying solo this week just because I can do whatever I want, but I don't want to be without him for the long term.

"He's a great guy," I finally say, breaking the comfortable silence that grew around us. I don't know what spurs me to start talking—maybe it's how open Paul was about losing Wilma, or maybe I just like connecting with people. "Tim tells me time and time again he'll do anything for me, and he does. He's only gone this week because he got a promotion at work and has to go to some classes."

For a moment, I think I feel Paul stiffen. We aren't anywhere near touching each other, but I swear that the energy in the air between us changes for just a moment, but then it's back to normal.

"Didn't you say he works in HR?"

I nod, then remember that he's watching the fire and not looking at me. "Yep. He likes it for the most part, but I don't know if I could do it."

"Why not? You seem like you would be great at getting along with people."

"Thanks, but I don't think I could fire anyone. I know that he's had to do that in the past, but he hates it. I don't think I could look someone in the eyes and do that, knowing full well that I'm ruining their life."

Paul doesn't say anything for a moment.

I take a bite of my cookie. "Anyway, that's why I can't do it. I know his boss wants him to take over all the hiring and firing, but he really doesn't want to."

"Sounds like he doesn't have a choice, though, does he? If he wants to keep his job and pay for you and the house, then he'll need to do whatever she says."

"Right. That's the problem, isn't it? We want to have kids, and now we have this gorgeous house, but he doesn't think he can ever fire someone again." I shrug, then realize I'm sharing more personal stuff than I meant to. "Anyway, that's enough about that. Getting fired has to be the worst."

"I'd imagine so." Paul stands up in a fluid motion and throws more wood onto the fire, then watches it flare up before turning back to me. "I'm glad you have him, Amy. Wives need husbands who are willing to do whatever it takes to keep them safe and protect their memory."

He's right, and I know Tim will do anything for me. Still, I don't know if it's the way Paul said it or the fact that I can't see his face with the fire behind him, but a shiver runs through me at his words.

17

PAUL

It took a long time for the fire to burn down enough for me to feel comfortable leaving it to go up to the main house. I should be going to the cottage to get some rest for another busy day of working in the yard tomorrow, but I want to make sure Amy got to bed okay.

My plans are changing, but I can't help that. Never in a million years did I think Tim would willingly leave Amy here on her own for a week. He wants to take care of her, wants to protect her, and what does he do?

He walks away, leaving her in this huge house all by herself, with only me here to make sure she's okay.

A shiver runs up my spine as I work my way silently through the walls of the house. It's still and quiet on the first floor, and I have a pretty good feeling Amy will be in bed already. She was yawning a lot before she finally made her way up to the house, and that was almost three hours ago. Excitement buzzes through my body as I unlock the door that leads into the foyer and step out into the house.

As a kid, I remember sneaking through the house all the time to spy on my parents and their friends. It was so much fun, ducking into the walls when someone was coming, creeping as quietly as possible so nobody knew you were there.

I had my own secret stash of books and snacks I'd snuck from the kitchen in the wall behind my bedroom. On special nights when my parents went to bed early, I would sneak back to my little nest in the walls and read for a few hours before finally crawling back to bed.

I loved to spy on my parents. I know all the little hidey-holes in the house, all the places where I can look out from the walls into the rooms, and how to move so silently that nobody will know I'm here.

Now, I climb the stairs to the second floor. I could move through the walls, but I saw how tired Amy was. I am certain she's sound asleep now. If she's not, and she does stir, I'll simply disappear into a fake door in the paneling.

But I don't want to be separated from her by a wall. I want to watch her without anything between us.

I have to decide what I'm going to do.

Skipping the steps that I know squeak, I work my way up to the second floor, then draw up short right outside her bedroom. The door is ajar, and I hold my breath as I push it open so I can see into the room.

Light from the moon brightens the space, but I can't see her well. I'm going to have to get closer.

I hold my breath as I cross the room.

I'm so quiet she doesn't stir, until I'm finally leaning right over her in the bed. Her hair fans out on the pillow like a halo, and her mouth is slightly open as she sleeps. I want to brush some stray hair back from her forehead, but I don't dare.

If I touch her, she'll wake.

I can only imagine how upset she would be if she found me here in her room. She wouldn't give me the chance to explain, to tell her I'm here for her, to save her, not hurt her. Someone has to protect her, even though that wasn't my original plan.

Clasping my hands together, I have to fight the urge to pull the blanket up higher under her chin and tuck her in. I want to take care of her, but she'll wake. I know it.

Instead, I turn and walk back across the room. I fully intend on leaving so she can get some sleep, but something catches my eye. On the dresser by the door are her wedding and engagement rings. I see them lying there, and I reach out, pushing them apart to get a better look at them.

I could take one. I could put it with her perfume and keep it for myself, but she'd notice it was missing right away. I don't want her to worry about things going missing, but I just can't help myself.

My fingers dance across her jewelry. It's all spread out on top of the dresser, some of it in little piles that are so disorganized I'm sure she won't miss some of it. Finally, my eyes land on the simple gold chain she was wearing the first time we met. She didn't have it on today, I would have noticed, so hopefully that means she won't notice it's gone immediately.

I slip it into my pocket before leaving her room. After casting one more glance in her direction to make sure she hasn't woken up, I crack the door behind me and go back downstairs and head to the kitchen. The sloppy joes she made for dinner were delicious, but I haven't had homemade cookies as often as I'd like besides the ones she made me the day we met.

Holly doesn't like to bake. She says she's watching her figure and doesn't want to overdo it on the treats. I find the container where Amy put the leftover cookies she'd brought and help myself to some of them before closing it and putting it back where it was.

She can't know I've been here, so I make sure nothing is

out of place before walking back to the door under the staircase in the foyer. Once it's closed behind me, I switch on my flashlight and make sure I lock the door so it can't be opened from inside the house, then head through the double walls to where I can climb back down the ladder.

Amy's safe and sleeping soundly, which is all that matters right now. I'm going to put her necklace in the small room where I have her perfume; then I'll go to bed, too.

I hurry down to where I have Wilma's shrine set up, excited to add Amy's necklace to it. When I'm there, I pause, fingering my wife's necklace as I think about what to do next.

It's not that I'm replacing Wilma with Amy. I honestly believe the two of them would have gotten along famously. Still, my fingers tremble a bit when I take Wilma's necklace and put Amy's in its place.

There. It's perfect.

There's no reason why I can't have things from both of them here. No reason why I can't love both of them. They're just so similar, both of them so kind and loving, so interested in what I have to say and in talking to me.

When I'm with Amy, it's like I have Wilma back. Then she's gone, and the pain I felt the moment my wife first forgot my name comes crashing down around me again.

Closing my eyes, I picture Wilma's kind eyes. Amy has them, too, a soft brown compared to Wilma's bright blue. But when she looks at me, it's like having my wife back for just a moment.

Just long enough.

If I'm going to protect Amy from Tim, I have to come up with a plan. To do that, I need some rest first. My body and my mind are both exhausted, and now I want to protect her, not hurt her, I have to rethink it all.

This was never the plan. I wasn't supposed to feel anything for Amy, and I certainly wasn't supposed to want to get closer to her, but I blame Tim for it all. He's the reason Wilma is dead, and now he left Amy here all by herself.

I could kill her right now and make him suffer, but there's no way I can make myself do that.

If I don't take care of her, who will?

18

TIM

I miss my wife. It's bizarre to be away from her for so long. In fact, I don't think she and I have ever spent more than a night or two apart, and after Sunday and Monday night without her across from me at the dinner table and then in my bed, I really miss her.

That's why I've had such a good idea.

I called her favorite restaurant and had to practically beg them to deliver to the house tonight. They weren't keen on going up the driveway and trying to find the house, which is understandable, but when I threw in a tip that almost doubled the actual order, they agreed to do it.

I'm going to order in room service so she and I can eat at the same time, and then I'm going to video chat with her so it will be like we're eating dinner together. It won't be the same after she gets off the computer and I have to go to bed on my own, but at least I'll be able to spend a little extra time with her.

Class is incredibly boring, and the only thing that would make this more bearable would be the possibility of seeing Amy tonight, so that's why I'm doing my best to make this happen. She's more of a planner than I am, so I'm sure she'd much rather I call her ahead of time and let her know what I'm planning, but I want to surprise her.

A video-chat date with my wife is just what I need to make it through the rest of this week.

Grinning to myself, I dress, putting on a nice shirt and even a tie. I don't have to put on actual pants, so I stay in the PJ pants I changed into as soon as class was over, but at least this way Amy will think I put a lot of effort into our little video date. I just hope she loves it.

As soon as I'm changed, I open my computer and get ready to call her, then check the time. The food should be delivered to the house in the next five minutes, as long as the restaurant does exactly what I asked. I told them over and over again how important the timing was, so hopefully they'll do their best.

One minute goes by, and I hear someone at my door. Hurrying to it, I take the tray of food from the man, press a twenty-dollar bill into his hand, then lock the door and put the food down by my computer.

Now.

Clicking the little button to video call my wife, I wait, anticipation making me nervous. She'll answer on her phone, I'm sure of it, unless she's writing late tonight. If that's the case, then she'll be on her computer. I just want to get her on the chat before her dinner arrives.

It rings multiple times and then cuts off.

Nonplussed, I hang up and call her again. If she was busy or in the bathroom, then she wouldn't have picked up, but I really want to make this happen for the two of us.

Again the ringing sound fills my hotel room, and again it abruptly cuts off.

"Where are you, Amy?" I ask, grabbing my phone to call her that way. I'm a little frustrated my date night isn't going as planned, but maybe the food was delivered early. I'll just tell her what I'm trying to do, and I'm sure she'll be on board. It won't be as big a surprise as it would have been had she picked up my video chat like I had hoped she would, but I can't get mad about that.

Something must have come up, but I have no doubt she'll drop whatever it is when she figures out I need her.

I start to get a little bit antsy when she doesn't answer her phone. Hanging up, I count to ten, then call her again, trying to ignore the growing pit in my stomach. It's not like I'm just at the office and can hop in the car, head home, and check on her. I'm hours away, and the only way to get someone to the house quickly if I'm really worried about her is to call the police.

And I can only imagine how pissed off she'd be if I did that.

Her phone clicks over to voicemail again, and I'm about to leave her a message asking her to call me back when suddenly there's a beeping in my ear. Relief floods through me when I see Amy's name on the screen, and I answer it as quickly as possible.

"Is everything okay?" The words are out of my mouth before I can stop them.

"I was going to ask you the same thing."

Is there a little bit of frustration underlying her words? It's hard for me to tell, and it's not like I'm going to ask her if she's really upset with me. "You kept my phone going crazy in my pocket. What's wrong? Are you hurt?"

"No, nothing like that." I look at the dinner I have set out on the desk for me to eat and slump down in my chair. "I'm sorry, I just really wanted to talk to you. Are you not at the house?"

"No, I'm not. Why?"

Now I feel like a fool. It seemed like a wonderful idea to

order in dinner for her and surprise her with it, but I can hear from the sharp edge to her words she's not at all thrilled with what I've done.

"Amy, I'm sorry. I ordered dinner to be delivered to you because I thought the two of us could have a video-chat date. But you're not at the house, so I'm not sure if they'll even leave it for you."

She pauses; then when she speaks again, her voice is a little softer. "Tim, that was really sweet of you, but I had no idea you were planning to do something like that. I made other plans for the evening."

"Oh, of course." It's not like I really thought she would sit around at home the entire time I was gone and miss me, but it's a little weird she has plans again. Last night was strange enough. A bonfire with our caretaker? I know Amy loves getting to know people, but he works for us. "What's the plan for the night? Did you call up some girlfriends to go out with?"

Another pause. "I'm actually having dinner with Paul."

"Oh." The word is hard and dry in my mouth, and I roll it around on my tongue like a rock before I finally manage to say it. "Well, that sounds really fun, doesn't it?"

"I thought so. Is that not okay? You sound upset."

Forcing myself to laugh, I shut my laptop. "No, of course not. I just wanted to see your gorgeous face, and I had no idea you were planning to eat dinner with him again."

"It wasn't really planned," she tells me. "He and I were talking about our favorite meals when we were younger, and we both love meatloaf. I told him you hate it, so I never make it, so he invited me to his cottage for dinner."

"I thought you said you weren't ever going to set foot in the cottage again after you called the cops." It's a low blow, and I should feel guilty about saying it to my wife, but I don't.

For some reason, I don't want her to have a nice dinner with Paul. I want her to have a nice dinner with me.

"It's different now that he lives down here, trust me. It's so cute, Tim. I don't know what I was ever afraid of."

She's down there now. The thought hits me hard, and I have to take a deep breath. Paul is older than her, and there's no way Amy would ever cheat on me. Still, it's unnerving to think about them eating dinner together in his cozy little cottage. There's hardly enough room in there to maneuver around the table, much less eat a meal with another person.

"I hope you have fun," I tell her, doing my best to keep my voice light. If Amy thinks that I don't want her having dinner with Paul, then I'll have to tell her why, and it sounds ridiculous even to me.

"We will! Thanks for trying to set up the date, Tim. I'm sorry it didn't work out. Maybe tomorrow?" She pauses. "If you want, I can go see if they dropped off the dinner?"

It's a nice offer, but I can tell from the tone of her voice that she doesn't really want to do that.

I shake my head even though she can't see me. "Don't worry about it tonight. And there's this dinner thing tomorrow night, so that won't work. Not to worry, Amy, I'll be home soon, okay?"

"Yep. Oh, you're ready?" She's not talking to me, and I can't help but feel a little irritated that she's having our conversation in front of Paul. He answers her, his voice low, but I can't make out what he's saying. When she speaks again, her words are meant for me. "No worries. Have a great night, Tim! I love you."

"I love you," I tell her, putting as much feeling and honesty into the words as I can, but she's already hung up.

What the hell is going on?

I was starving just a few minutes ago, but now I replace the lid on my food and push it to the side. I really just wanted to spend some time with my wife even though I'm not there, but she sure isn't sitting around waiting on me, is she?

It's stupid, but I suddenly don't want to be in my room, eating my sad meal alone while she's hanging out with someone else. Who cares that it's just the caretaker? Who cares how much older than us he is? I don't like it.

My mind is made up. There was a group of people going out for dinner and drinks tonight, and I bet if I hurry down to the lobby, I can catch them. I throw on some real pants and grab my phone and room key before locking up and walking quickly to the elevator.

I'm not the only one in this marriage who knows how to have fun.

19

AMY

I have no idea what got into Tim last night, but to say he was irritated about me having dinner with Paul would be an understatement. He acted like we were in high school and I had made the huge mistake of talking to another guy while we were dating.

It's not like anything would ever happen between Paul and me, anyway. Not only is he much older than me, but I don't think he's that kind of guy, and I'm definitely not that type of person. Sure, he was super interested in everything I had to say, and it was obvious he was paying attention to my answers because he asked lots of relevant follow-up questions, but I never felt like he was hitting on me.

I just felt like he honestly wanted to get to know me, and that was really nice. It's not that Tim and I don't talk and don't connect, but he's so often stressed out with work that he just falls silent during dinner and then turns on the TV after we're done eating, leaving me to clean up the kitchen.

I take a deep breath, trying to calm my brain. This is supposed to be our fresh start. We moved out of the apartment where Tim made his big mistake before. He promised me a fresh start was all we needed, so why don't things feel different?

I'd honestly thought moving here would give us a big project to work on together and bring us closer, but as soon as he got the idea of hiring a caretaker in his mind, there was no slowing him down. Paul's here now, probably to stay, and I have to admit I really like it.

I'm up early this morning so I can do some writing before the sun comes up. Normally I'd still be snoozing and then stumbling around the house with a cup of coffee clutched in my hand for an hour before even considering sitting down and working, but Paul promised me he would show me how to finish trimming back the roses.

He told me it's normally something that needs to be done in spring, not fall, but the garden is in such disrepair that it's better to start the job now than to shock the roses in the spring with huge cuts that will make it harder for them to come back.

I can't wait.

Rather than being handed clippers and pointed in the direction of the garden with Tim yelling encouragement at me, Paul is actually going to take time and show me what to do. It's exciting that he's willing to spend a little more time teaching me than just doing it himself. I'll never spend as much time as he does working in the garden, but it will be nice to have a better idea of what I'm doing out there.

As I brush my teeth, I check my phone to see if I missed anything last night. I'm half hoping Tim will have sent me a text at bedtime like he did the first night he was in Raleigh, but there isn't anything there from him.

"Cool, Tim, cool," I mutter to myself, then tap on a bright icon. Instagram is my weakness, and I know scrolling through it this early in the morning puts me at a very real risk of getting sucked into a rabbit hole instead of getting started on work, but I still want to see if I missed anything.

Probably not. Nobody puts anything real on social media. It's all perfectly curated to make other people think your life is wonderful. Still, I can't help but flick my thumb on the screen, sending pictures flying until I see my husband.

But it's not just Tim.

I don't know who the woman in the picture is, or why her head's leaning on his shoulder. They're both laughing; then I see he's holding a microphone in his hand, his other arm held out in front of him so he can snap the selfie.

It's happening again.

I spit into the sink and calmly rinse my toothbrush, still staring at the picture. The woman isn't tagged in the post, but it doesn't take me long to figure out exactly who she is since she so helpfully commented on the post with a lot of red hearts and smiley faces.

Sitting on the edge of the bed, I tap on her screen name. She's also in HR, apparently, and at the same conference as my husband, which explains why I don't know her. What that doesn't explain is why she thought it would be a good idea to take this picture with him and then comment on it.

I flick through her pictures, getting more and more agitated, then screenshot the post Tim made in case he tries to delete and deny it. As soon as I hear the soft click my phone makes when it takes a screenshot, I pause.

What am I doing? Do I really think my husband would do something bad and then try to hide it from me? *Yes, I do.* But that's not who Tim is anymore, right, so why am I so worried about it? *Because he broke my trust once already.*

Now I can't help but wonder what else the two of them got up to last night. I check the timestamp on the picture.

No, not last night. *This morning.* This was posted at one this morning, probably right when the bar was closing down for the night. And here I was thinking he was upset with me for having meatloaf with Paul while he was out living it up with Susie.

Before I can stop myself, I text the screenshot to my husband.

Care to explain this???

Even though I really hope there's a logical explanation for what I just saw, I'm not able to come up with one. Tim will have to explain it to me.

If he can.

FOUR HOURS LATER, I'm standing in the garden with Paul, learning how to look for the right number of leaves on the roses before making a cut. I'm glad he's teaching me this because otherwise I would have come out here and just started hacking the roses down to the ground.

"You have to be careful when choosing where to cut," he tells me, reaching out to adjust where my clippers are placed yet again. "And it helps if your head is in the game. What's going on, Amy? You seem really distracted."

I exhale hard, then hesitate. Do I tell him? Can I really open up to this man, or will that just color his perception of Tim when my husband finally gets back? The last thing I want to do is make Paul think Tim is a terrible guy, especially since my husband is technically his boss, but every time I close my eyes, I picture Tim getting so cozy with that other woman.

Susie.

"It must be hard having Tim gone. Is that it?"

Paul's voice is so kind and compassionate that I can't help

the tears that spring to the corners of my eyes. I hate that I'm going to cry, but I feel them burning there, and I angrily reach up and wipe them away, rubbing my rough gloves across my cheeks.

Maybe if Tim had responded to my text, I wouldn't be so upset, but I haven't heard from him yet this morning. I hope he didn't make a terrible mistake last night.

"I just miss him," I say, giving Paul a nod. That's it. That's all I'm going to say. He was married, so he'll understand how hard it can be to be away from your spouse.

"That's not all, though, is it, Amy? You're so kind, so loving. What did he do?" He reaches out and lightly squeezes my shoulder.

I'm suddenly overcome with the urge to turn to him and let him hug me. He's not my dad, and I know that, but the way he's treating me right now makes me feel like he cares about me the way a father might. My dad left my mom shortly after I was born, and even though I'm not related to Paul, I can't help but want to share what's been going on with him.

"He went out for dinner and drinks last night and posted a picture of himself with some woman," I say, ripping one glove off with my teeth and letting it fall to the ground so I can grab my phone to show Paul. There's a voice in the back of my head telling me to stop before I really throw Tim under the bus, but I can't help it. "There she is."

He gently takes my phone from me and looks at the screen, raising one eyebrow as he does. "He was out with her instead of in his hotel room missing you?"

I nod, taking a shuddering breath. There's a little voice in the back of my mind reminding me that I was outside having dinner with Paul instead of staying in the house missing Tim, but I push that voice away.

"Then he's lost his mind." Paul hands me back my phone.

I turn off the screen without looking at the picture again. I don't want to see the two of them grinning up at the camera together.

"But he's good to you, Amy. He loves you. You don't really think he would do anything to jeopardize your marriage, do you?"

Do I?

Up until this morning I never would have thought he'd do anything to hurt me or make me think he doesn't love me again, but right now I'm not sure what I think. We got through the hard times, didn't we? This is supposed to be easy now that we've found our fresh start.

Still, I'm hurt, and I know it's probably silly, but I can't help it.

"I know he loves me," I say, and I hate that my voice trembles, but I can't stop it, "but then why did he post this picture?"

Paul is silent. "Was he upset about anything when you talked to him last night?"

I pause, unwilling to tell this kind man the truth. There's no way I can tell him that Tim was upset that Paul and I were having dinner together last night. It would seriously break his heart to think he might be part of the problem between me and my husband, so I do the only thing I can.

I lie.

"No, he was fine. He didn't mention anything about going out, but he was in a good mood."

"Well, then." Paul looks up at the sky and sighs. "I don't know what to tell you, Amy. But I saw the way he looked at you when he was home. He loves you, and you're worth more than a hundred of those drunk Susies. Have you asked him what happened last night?"

"He didn't respond." My voice is flat, and I realize how bad this all sounds. My husband was out on the town until the wee hours of the morning, drinking and partying with another woman, and then when I asked him about it, all I get is radio silence.

"I'm sure there's a reasonable explanation," Paul tells me. "I don't know what it is, but I'm sure he has one. I just hope you don't get hurt, Amy." He gives me a kind grin and then squeezes my shoulder again.

I want a hug, but I'm not going to ask for one. "Thanks, Paul. Sorry for burdening you with this."

"Oh, no, you are not a burden. And if Tim ever tells you you are or makes you feel like you are, then he and I need to have some words. Don't let him bring you down. You have a gorgeous spirit, Amy, remember that." With that, he turns and resumes work on the roses.

I watch him for a moment before picking up my glove and grabbing my clippers to help him.

Paul is right. I don't know what's going on with Tim, but I do know I'm worth more than how he's making me feel. If he did something terrible last night, then we'll have to face that later, but right now I'm enjoying myself.

I'm spending time with someone who actually makes me feel good about who I am.

And if Tim were to call me right now, I'm not entirely sure I would answer.

20

PAUL

Amy lied to me, but I forgive her for it. She only did it to protect Tim. That's what a good spouse is supposed to do. They're supposed to do or say whatever it takes to protect their partner. Husbands should certainly not go out with other women drinking while their sweet wife is home alone.

What Tim and Amy don't know, and can't ever know, is that Amy wasn't alone. I watched her last night, making sure she got to bed safely. I made sure she stayed asleep, that bad dreams didn't keep her up.

It got chilly out last night, and she had her window open. There wasn't any way I was going to let her freeze with the cool night air coming into her room. When I came back to check on her after midnight this morning and saw that she'd kicked off her blanket, I did the one thing I knew I could do to help her.

I came out of the walls and carefully tugged it back up over her. She didn't even shift in her sleep. It was nice to sit in her room for a while and watch her, making sure she was okay. Tim certainly isn't doing anything to protect her and keep her safe, and someone has to do it.

I'm the only one who can.

Now I'm tired, but it was all worth it. I'm taking my job of keeping her safe very seriously, which is a little ironic.

At first, I'd thought the best way to make Tim suffer for making it impossible for me to take care of Wilma was to take Amy from him, but now I know that's wrong. I want to save her from him. He's evil, and he'll end up hurting her if I don't protect her.

Just look at what happened this morning when we were cutting back the roses. She was distraught that he had been out with another woman. It killed me to see the look on her face when she showed me the picture, but it's not like I can do anything right now. Tim is safe and sound in Raleigh, doing whatever the hell he wants, and his poor wife is here all alone.

Leaving my cottage, I glance up at the house. I can see her office window from here, but there's a glare across the glass from the sun, so it's impossible to tell if she's working right now or not. Still, I have a feeling she is. We took longer than necessary to finish the roses because I wanted her to feel free to open up more about Tim.

She did, telling me about how thrilled she'd been when they were able to buy this house. The two of them haven't been married very long, and part of me thinks this house was more Amy's idea than Tim's. She loves it the way I always have, loves the amazing staircase, the huge kitchen, all of the gardens. Her eyes lit up when we were finished pruning and even more so when I told her she'd done a good job.

When she finally left, she told me she was going to get something to eat and then do some work on the computer. I could slip into the house to check on her, but I don't see a reason to right now. Instead of walking around the house to sneak in and find out where she is, I decide to call my daughter. I've put it off long enough.

Holly picks up on the second ring, her voice happy but tired. "Dad, hey, how's it going? You still enjoying the little cottage or getting jealous of the big house?"

"The cottage is great," I assure her. "But I wanted to let you know there's been a change of plans. It's about Amy."

"Amy? Really? Hold on, let me shut my office door." I hear her moving around for a moment. "Okay, let's hear it." She exhales hard, and I can picture her mind going a million miles a minute as she tries to figure out what's going on. "What is it, Dad? What's going on with Amy?"

I can't tell her. Not yet. I have to lead her there, have to get her to come to the realization on her own, if possible. "Tell me, what did you think of Tim?"

"He's arrogant. Devoted to his job. The house was more Amy's idea than his, but she managed to get him on board."

She's right. He is arrogant, and instead of being devoted to his wife, he pours all his energy and time into his job. No wonder Amy looks so sad when I mention him. No wonder she's willing to have dinner with me while he's gone and only lights up when the conversation moves away from her marriage.

I see it all now.

"But why did you just change the subject to Tim?" There's clear accusation in her voice.

I flinch even though her words can't actually hurt me. "She's kind, Holly. She deserves more than him."

"Deserves more than him? She married him, and I'd say that means she deserves exactly what she's going to get. I thought you were going to get justice for Mom." My daughter's voice is suddenly flat and hard, but I'm not going to let her words get to me. "I thought you were going to use Amy to show Tim how much it hurt when we lost Mom."

"I'm going to make him suffer," I promise her. "Don't you worry about that. But Amy is innocent. I know it."

She's silent; then I hear her drumming her fingers on her desk. "Innocent people don't marry someone like Tim."

There's ice in the air between us. I know she's pissed, but I also know that she has to listen to me.

"Trust me," I tell her. "Please, Holly, you have to trust me on this one. The plan changed. My plan changed. I'm not going to hurt her just to bring him down, got it?"

"No, that was the plan," she says. "Hurting Amy to make Tim suffer. Don't change it. You're making a mistake even thinking about it."

Just then I see movement in Amy's office window. She's struggling to get it to open. I can see her trying to push it up and failing.

"I'm not," I tell my daughter, still watching Amy struggle with the window. I want to help her. Someone should be up there to help her with anything she needs. It's not right that such a kind person like her is married to someone who doesn't care about her. "Don't try to change my mind."

Before she can respond, I hang up, then whistle as I walk quickly to the house. Things with Holly aren't settled yet, but I hate seeing Amy struggle. I'm not going to knock on the front door and offer to help her. No, that would be too up front, and I don't want her to realize I was watching the house. Instead, I'm going to grab the wheelbarrow from where I left it under her office window and take it back to the garden.

She can call out to me if she wants my help.

I'm just grabbing the wheelbarrow when I hear her sweet voice. "Paul! Hey, are you busy? I can't get this window to open!" Her voice is muffled, but she's calling me loud enough that I can still hear her.

I stop and look up, shielding my eyes from the sun. "Where are you?" I call, like I don't know.

"Second floor! If you don't mind taking a look at it, I'll be right down to let you in."

Grinning to myself, I walk over to the front door.

Sure enough, a moment later she's there, opening the door and smiling sheepishly at me. "I'm so sorry to bother you, Paul, but the window is painted shut or something. I can get one of the windows in the bedroom open, but there are a few of them I can't open by myself. Do you mind?"

"Lead the way," I tell her, stepping through the door.

She does, and I follow her up to her office. It's strange being in this room with her here and awake. I only get to visit the various rooms in the house when she's asleep and won't hear me puttering around.

Pausing in front of the window, I take in the view. It's gorgeous during the day. At night, everything is dark and obscured by shadows. From here she can see part of the cottage, but not its door, which pleases me. While I want to be able to keep track of her coming and going, I don't want her to be able to do the same to me.

"I think it's painted shut," Amy says, pointing.

"Nope, just a little bit swollen. Any paint that was on the windows has chipped off or flaked away." I point to show her what I mean. "All we need to do is force it up, and you should be good. If it keeps causing problems, then I'll come back and shave the wood down, but I really think I can take care of it now. Move your laptop, okay?"

"Oh, right." Amy grabs her computer and water cup.

I step forward, bracing my hands on the sill before planting my feet and shoving upward. At first, the window doesn't want to move. It holds fast, and I adjust my grip, pushing again. There's a slight pause, like everything is hanging on by a thread; then the window groans and slides up.

"There you go," I say, stepping back. "It'll need to be worked up and down a few times to break it back in, and like I said, I can do more work on it if I need to, but I know you want to get back to writing." My eyes flick around her desk and fall on a stack of pages I just noticed. "Are you working on a book?"

Her face flames, and she puts her computer down, reaching out to rest her fingers on the papers. "Actually, yeah. Tim's the only other person who knows about it because I don't know if it's any good, but I've always wanted to write a book, so I've been working on it. It's what I like to work on before bed."

So that's what she was working on last night. I'd watched her for a while, watched as she hunched over her computer, typing away furiously. Of course, I hadn't been able to get nearly close enough to see what she was writing, but her working on a book makes sense. She'd been incredibly excited as she was writing, I could tell that even from looking through a hole in the wall across the room.

"That's amazing, Amy," I tell her. "Seriously. There are tons of people who say they want to do just that and then never do. You have to be really proud."

"I am, thanks." She grins at me. "It's fun to write. I'll probably put it aside and never do anything with it, but I still can say I wrote a book."

"You won't ask Tim to read it?"

She pauses, then shakes her head. "No, he's not a big reader like I am. I'm not sure if he'd be interested."

Of course he wouldn't be interested. He doesn't deserve Amy. He has no idea how incredible she is, and he's just taking advantage of her. I do my best to keep my frustration hidden so Amy won't know how I feel about her husband.

"I'd love to. Read it, that is, when you're finished with it. If that's okay with you."

She chews on her lower lip and then looks up at me. "Really? You don't think it's stupid?"

"That you're writing a book?" I shake my head. "Not at all. I think it's awesome, and I'd love to be the first person to really support you."

"Okay. Yeah." She nods, then pats the stack of pages by her computer like pointing them out to me will stop her from changing her mind. "Yeah, I'd like that, thanks. When it's done. Be kind, okay? I'm close to the end, and I think I can finish it before you go."

"I'm never anything else, especially not to you." Grinning at her, I take a step back. "I'll let you get back to it, okay? And don't think I'm going to slack off reading all afternoon when you do give it to me. It will be for my own enjoyment when I'm relaxing in the evening."

"You're the best." She hesitates, then speaks again, faster this time. "Do you want to come up here for dinner tonight? I don't want you to feel like you have to, but I'm enjoying our meals."

"I'd love to," I tell her. I know she's hurting from the way Tim has been treating her. I know that that's the reasonable explanation for why she wants me to come to dinner tonight, but I don't care. It has nothing to do with her really enjoying my company, as much as I wish it did, but I'm still going to come and enjoy eating with her.

Tim is a terrible person and a terrible husband. Amy needs to see that she's much better off without him.

Because soon she really will be.

21

TIM

I've been avoiding my phone all day. I'd like to say it's because I'm so devoted to my work and the classes and lectures I'm taking here in Raleigh, but that would be a lie. I just don't want to read the text message from Amy again.

I know she's mad and hurt, but I don't know what to say to her. Nothing happened with Susie last night besides the two of us singing our hearts out at karaoke. We drank, we ate, we sang, and then I stupidly posted a selfie of the two of us to my Instagram where Amy could see it.

Was there part of me that posted it because I wanted her to see it? Maybe, but there's no way in hell I'd ever admit that to her. I can only imagine how much it would hurt her to know there was even a tiny part of me last night that thought it was a good idea to post a picture with another woman.

Still, she saw it. I took the post down this morning after I saw her text to me, but she's screenshotted it, which means it's not something I can try to explain away or pretend didn't happen. She knows, and now that I haven't responded to her, she probably thinks I'm guilty of something even worse.

I'm not. I swear I'm not. We had a great time last night, but now I know how to draw the line.

I'm back in the hotel lobby, and I sit down on a sofa there to make the call to my wife. While I should probably do this in the privacy of my own room to make sure I'm not interrupted, I don't want to be alone while I call her. She's going to be angry, but if she realizes I'm in a public place, then it's much less likely she's going to throw a major fit.

She won't want to embarrass me and herself. Sure, she'll be mad, but I don't think this will turn into a really huge problem if I go ahead and take care of it now.

I've only ever felt this nervous calling Amy once before, and that was when I called her the first time to see if she would go out to dinner with me. She'd sounded so excited when she answered, and I just hope there's one bit of that same excitement in her voice today.

But there isn't.

"Tim, you're back from the dead," she says, her voice dry.

I swallow hard and wait to hear what else she's going to say, but she doesn't speak, so I know I don't have a choice. "Hey, Amy, are you okay?"

"Am I okay? You can't honestly be that stupid, Tim." Her words hurt, which is exactly what she wants, I'm sure of it.

"I'm sorry about the picture," I say, suddenly wishing I had decided to do this in my room. Maybe it would be better to face her screaming and crying in the privacy of my own room than to deal with a calm and angry wife in the lobby of a hotel. "I want you to know that nothing happened between the two of us."

A woman walking by glances over at my words and gives a little shake of her head like she can't believe what she's hearing.

My face burns, and I hurry for the stairwell. I'll lose Amy

if I get in the elevator, but I'm hoping I can make it up to my room without the call dropping if I take the stairs.

"That's no consolation, Tim. You looked pretty drunk, and I know you have to be drunk to even consider karaoke. How do you expect me to believe you?"

Those are good points, but I'm not going to admit that to her. I burst out into the hall and turn towards my room, walking fast and thinking faster. "I love you. I went out with some friends from class and ended up drinking more than I meant to, but it wasn't like I was out with just Susie, okay? We were with a group."

"The group must have been huge if you couldn't get everyone in the picture," she says dryly.

I stop in front of my door and shove my hand into my pocket for the key.

"And why has it taken you until five this evening to answer my text? It doesn't look good, Tim."

"Tim!" A voice from down the hall makes me turn. Susie is walking towards me, practically beaming as she waves her arm high above her head. "There you are! Did you forget we wanted to go to karaoke together tonight before the group dinner?"

"Is that Susie?" Amy's voice is harsh in my ear. "It is, isn't it? You guys have a date tonight, huh?"

"Listen, Amy," I say, holding up one finger to Susie to try to get her to stop. She's not calling out to me anymore, but she's still walking towards me, eating up the space between us. "I don't remember making these plans, okay? Don't think for a moment I would do something like that."

"So you don't remember setting a date with your karaoke buddy, but you can promise me that you do remember not sleeping with her? You can't have it both ways, Tim." She hangs up.

I groan, closing my eyes and taking a deep breath.

"Tim, aren't you excited?" Susie grabs my arm and grins at me. She has on the same rich perfume she did last night but has changed into something more casual after our day of classes. Her shirt is more low-cut than the one she was wearing last night, and all I can do is say a little prayer of thanks she wasn't wearing it in the picture.

"So excited," I lie. "I just need to change, and then I'll be ready." Digging my key out of my pocket, I open the door and turn to her, keeping my body in the doorway so she can't follow me in. "Give me ten minutes, okay? Maybe fifteen. I'll meet you downstairs."

After I close and lock the door, I lean against it with a sigh and dial Amy again.

"Come on, pick up," I say, starting to pace around the room. "Don't screen me, Amy."

But she does. Not just once, but five times, before I finally give up and leave her a voicemail.

"Listen, Amy, I'm sorry about that. Nothing crazy happened last night, I promise you. I love you. I wouldn't ever do anything to hurt you again." I pause, unsure of how to get my point across. No, I don't remember all of the night, but I know for sure I wouldn't ever do anything to hurt my wife. "Please call me. It doesn't matter what time of the day or night you want to talk, I'll pick up."

When I hang up, I rub my temples. They're absolutely pounding, and I exhale a shaky breath as I put my phone in my pocket after making sure the ringer is turned to high.

Even as I feel guilty, though, a wave of anger washes over me. I'm not the only one out spending time with other people. Amy might get mad at me for spending time with Susie, but she's having dinner with Paul every single night.

Who's to say she's not doing that right now? I have no reason to believe that she's not going to have dinner with him again for a third night in a row. I might be out with friends, and sure, some of them are women, but at least I'm not inviting them into our house to eat.

"Tim?" Susie's voice floats through the door, and she knocks hard on it to get my attention. "If we want to sit close to the karaoke stage, then we'll need to get a move on, or all the good tables will be gone by the time we get there."

Screw it. I'm a little annoyed with Susie for coming to my room when I told her I'd meet her downstairs, but right now I don't care. My own wife doesn't want to talk to me right now and would probably rather eat dinner with our caretaker. If I want to go out and sing karaoke with a new friend I've made, then I'm going to do that, and I refuse to feel bad about it.

22

AMY

Even though I know I'm alone in the house, I swear I can feel someone's eyes on me. I'm washing dishes in the kitchen sink, trying to calm down after my conversation with Tim, but it's almost impossible. How he could be so calm on the phone when he had to know he was killing me by going out with Susie again tonight is beyond me.

Keeping my hands in the warm sudsy water, I turn, my eyes searching the wall behind me. It's silly to think anyone is behind me, watching me, but I swear I felt a gaze on my back. Of course, nobody is in the room, but that doesn't stop the strange feeling of someone watching me from creeping up my spine.

Hurriedly, I pull the sink stopper and watch the water swirl down the drain before quickly drying my hands on a towel and going upstairs. Even though I'm a little creeped out right now, I still want to get ready for my dinner with Paul. I never put on jewelry this morning, and I feel naked without something on. In my bedroom I pause by my dresser, my fingers dancing over the pieces that are there.

But the thin gold necklace Tim gave me when we first started dating is gone.

"Weird," I say, scooting a few other necklaces out of the way to keep looking. "I would have sworn it was right here the other day."

I can't remember when I wore it last, but it's definitely not here. Tim would probably tell me I stuck it wherever I accidentally put my perfume after we first moved in, so there's no way I'm going to tell him it's missing. Wherever it is, it's going to have to wait until after dinner with Paul. He'll be up at the house soon, so I grab a different necklace, clasp it around my neck, then head back to the kitchen.

Easy is the name of the game tonight, and I have no doubt Paul won't care that we're having leftover spaghetti and salads. I think about pulling out my leftover Chinese, but decide selfishly to leave that for later when I'm looking for a quick snack. It only takes me a minute to get everything out of the fridge, and I have to admit that chopping up the veggies for the salad feels pretty good. I'm angry at my husband, and each satisfying chop of the knife against the cutting board helps release some of my pent-up aggression.

But the strange feeling of being watched is still here. I've never felt my skin crawl before and always thought it was a strange expression, but I swear I can feel it now.

It's weird to feel on edge in your own house, but this place hasn't been ours long enough to really feel like home. Between stuff going missing and the weird teacup incident when we first moved in, I guess I haven't really relaxed here yet.

I put my knife down on the cutting board and walk to the wall opposite to where I was standing. Nobody is in the kitchen. There aren't even any photos on the wall that might make me feel like someone's eyes were on me, so then why am I so uncomfortable? Running my hands along the wall, I walk the length of the kitchen in one direction, then come back to the middle to go the other way.

The walls are smooth, but then I see a hole right above where I'm standing. I can reach up and put my finger in it, but it's too high for me to see through it, so I grab a kitchen chair and push it over to the wall.

My nerves are on edge as I stand on the chair and lightly brush my fingers across the hole. Taking a deep breath, I look in, afraid someone is going to be staring back at me.

But that's impossible. No one will be there, and surely there isn't even enough space for someone to get behind the wall. Still, when I look into the hole, my stomach is twisted hard in knots from the fear of what I might find.

Nothing. I see nothing but darkness, but I do feel cool air flowing through the hole. Reaching back up, I stick my finger into the hole, trying to see how much space there is back there. A sharp knock at the door makes me jump, and I swear, yanking my finger back from the wall and hopping down from the chair.

I was a little creeped out from when I thought I was being watched, but I rub my hands up and down my arms to calm myself. *It's just Paul.* Nobody was watching me through the wall. My overactive imagination is running away with me again, and I need to figure out how to turn that part of my brain off.

Hurrying over to the door, I swing it open, a smile on my face. It's not fake, either. I'm really happy to see him.

"I brought brownies," he tells me, thrusting a plate into my hands. "My daughter made them over the weekend, so they've been in the freezer, but I think they're still good, especially if you have milk to dunk them in."

"They look amazing," I say, gesturing him in with a sweep of my hand. "Thank you for bringing them. I was just finishing up the salad, and you'd never believe it, it's the

weirdest thing, but I'd swear someone was watching me."
The words spill out of me faster than I meant them to.

"Probably an angel," Paul remarks immediately.

I pause, surprised, then turn to him. "I didn't know you're
religious."

"There's a lot we don't know about each other, Amy. But
yes, I believe in God and His justice. It's hard not to when you
go through losing your spouse like I did."

His voice is softer than it's been in the past, and I
suddenly feel bad, like maybe I'm pushing him too hard. But
he's the one who brought up angels, while here I was
thinking there was someone in the house watching me.

How could I be so insensitive? I've heard dozens of stories
about people finding religion and turning to God when they
go through a huge emotional crisis. I've just never been faced
with anything like that, so hopefully it makes sense that I
would think it something surprising.

"Angels would be fine," I say, leading him to the kitchen
and quickly plating our meals.

He waits for me to sit at the table and then joins me.

"You know the feeling I'm talking about though, right?
Like there's something or someone right behind you, keeping
an eye on you, yet you can't see them?" I give a little shiver
and wait for him to respond.

I don't want to mention the fact that two things have gone
missing since we moved in. I can only imagine how crazy
Paul would think I was if I told him that. I just want to figure
out where I put my perfume and my necklace. Tim is
convinced I misplaced my perfume, and maybe he's right.

But what if he's not?

"Are you chilled? You keep shivering." Paul's about to take
a bite of spaghetti but honestly looks worried as he waits for
me to respond.

"I'm fine," I tell him. "Nothing a nice warm dinner can't

help." As we both fall on our food, I can't help but think about what Tim is doing right now. Is he out with Susie? Are they drinking beer and singing karaoke?

Is he doing more than just singing?

My fingers itch to check my phone and stalk his social media, but I refuse to do that. How insane would Paul think I was if I couldn't even have a single meal without checking up on my husband?

"Is Tim having a good time in Raleigh?" Paul asks.

His question is innocent, but I still jerk my head up to look at him.

"He's halfway done, right? He's probably made some good friends and is out with them rather than sitting alone in his hotel room."

I wish that was what he was doing.

"I think so," I tell him, choosing my words carefully. The last thing I want to do is color Paul's perception of my husband. I probably already did that, and I feel bad about it, but it's not like I can go back in time and change things now. "He's tired, as you can imagine, and really wants to get home."

"I'm sure he does. It would be impossible for me to think he'd rather spend time with anyone other than you. I can see how in love the two of you are, Amy."

"Thank you," I say, then stuff my mouth with some spaghetti. I love Tim, and I know he loves me, but his behavior this week is something else. I don't know what to say or think about it, and I'm afraid if I approach Tim with it, he'll just get defensive.

Taking a deep breath, I carefully guide the conversation back to safer waters. Paul and I spend the next hour talking about flowers and garden design, and we even sketch out what we think we can do with an empty garden plot by the side of the house on a piece of paper.

By the time he leaves, I'm exhausted, but still have dishes to clean up.

Humming to myself, I wash the dishes, then leave them in the dish drainer to drip dry overnight. Normally, I'd dry them off, but I'm really tired. I'm about to leave the kitchen when I remember the hole in the wall. Turning back to the dish drainer, I grab the long wooden spoon I used to stir the spaghetti and walk over to the chair I left up against the wall.

"There isn't going to be any space back there," I tell myself, carefully inserting the end of the wooden spoon into the hole. Still, I'm nervous as I push it through.

It doesn't hit the back of the wall.

"What in the world? How much space is back there?" The bowl of the spoon rests on the wall, the handle having traveled all the way back beyond the hole, but I still have no idea how deep it is back there.

Something could live in the walls, I guess. That thought is horrifying.

It's probably just a rat. There's no way anything bigger than that would be watching me.

Right?

23

PAUL

I couldn't help myself. I had to watch Amy after our dinner, had to make sure she tidied up and went to bed at a reasonable hour. I know she's all torn up over the way Tim is treating her, but what I can't tell her is that he just isn't worth it.

She could do much better. He's evil, through and through, which is something that I've known for a long time but she hasn't quite figured out yet. As much as I want to protect her from him, the only thing I can do right now is sit back and watch. I can't get involved, not yet, not while he's gone.

I can't let Amy know I'm watching and listening.

My heart sank when she found the hole in the kitchen wall. They're scattered throughout the house, all of them high enough on the walls that you have to actively look for them to find them. I didn't think she'd notice it there for a while yet, but she's now yanked a chair over to the wall again and started poking into the hole with the handle of a wooden spoon, and all I can do is watch.

This is not good.

She mutters to herself, and I pull away from where I'm

watching her, panic rising in my chest. She's not the brightest person in the world, but if she's found one hole, she's sure to find another. If she gets any inkling about what's going on in the walls of her house, then I'm sure she'll do everything she can to stop it.

I can't let her find out the truth.

I hurry through the walls, moving as quickly as I can without making any noise, finally dropping down into the space under the house. Normally I'd take time to lock up and ensure everything was closed up tight, but right now I'm in too much of a rush, and I run around the side of the house.

It started raining a little bit, and the grass is damp. I slip once but manage to keep myself from falling and push harder as I make my way up to the house.

By the time I reach the front porch, I'm panting, and I grab the railing to catch my breath for a moment. The last thing I want is for Amy to wonder why I'm out of breath. I have to get in there and stop her from poking into the walls.

What if she decides to do something drastic, like tear down a wall? I'm not entirely sure I can see her doing that, but people do crazy things when they're all worked up, and she's definitely close to the edge right now.

Gasping for air, I suck one more deep breath into my lungs and then go stand on the porch, waiting just a moment before I knock on the door. I can't hear any movement inside the house, but I have no doubt she's scurrying around, trying to figure out what she's going to do next.

One moment goes by, then another, and I'm lifting my hand to knock again when she throws the door open. Amy always looks calm and put together, but right now that facade has dropped, and she looks terrified. I eyeball her, wondering how much more she can take before she loses it, but before I can spin a lie about why I'm standing on her front porch, she motions me inside.

"Paul, please don't think I'm insane," she tells me, plucking at my sleeve, "but I think there was something in the walls earlier."

I'm reluctant as I follow her into the kitchen. The chair is still pushed up against the wall right where I saw it last, and I swallow hard as she points at the wall.

"There. There's a hole in the wall, Paul, and I swear something was watching me through it." Her voice is high and tight, and I reach out without thinking, putting my hand on her shoulder to try to calm her down.

"A hole?" I ask, and when she nods, I walk over to the chair and carefully step up on it. I have to make it look like I'm really investigating what she's telling me. Of course, I know where the hole is, but I still run my hand over the wall, pretending to look for it. I know where all the holes in the house are, but when my finger catches on it, I manage to look surprised.

"See?" She's excited and nervous, a dangerous combination, and I glance back at her. "Look in it. Oh, here." She thrusts the wooden spoon at me, and I weigh it in my hand like I'm not sure what to do with it. "You can stick it in the hole," she tells me, gesturing. "It'll let you see just how much space there is behind the wall."

"Amy, have you been doing this all day?" I ask, carefully turning and slipping the spoon into the hole. It sinks all the way in, just like the two of us knew it would.

"No, I saw it after you left. Someone was watching me through it. Or something, rather."

"You really think so?" I frown, then press my eye up against the hole. Of course, it's too dark in between the walls to see anything, but I make a good show of looking. "How would someone get in the walls?"

For the first time since she opened the door and saw me on her front porch, she sounds unsure of herself. "I don't know, exactly, but I promise you, Paul, I felt someone watching me. This house ... I think it's haunted."

Handing her the spoon, I get back down off the chair. "You believe in ghosts? Because I believe in rats. It's old and drafty, and I'd bet you anything that a family of critters set up shop in here before you and Tim moved in, and now don't want to leave."

Her shoulders slump, just a little bit, but enough for me to notice. "You really think it's just rats?"

"I do." I give her a firm nod. "It's the most logical explanation, isn't it?" I hate lying to her. She reminds me so much of my Wilma that I want to pull her to me and hug her. I want to take care of her and make her feel better, not make her feel even worse, but I don't have a choice right now.

"Yes, but it didn't *feel* like a rat watching me, if that makes sense. It felt ... more sinister, I guess, I don't know. And that doesn't explain everything else, either."

"What do you mean?"

She shakes her head and slowly walks over to the counter to put the wooden spoon away. "It's silly, Paul, pretend I never said anything."

"No, if you're worried about something, then I want to help. I promised Tim the first day I met you two I would keep you safe while he was gone, and I'm not doing a great job of that if you're afraid while you're in your own house." Picking up the chair, I carry it over to the table and put it back where it belongs. She can still move it to look through the hole again, but I don't think she will.

Not tonight, anyway.

"It's ridiculous, but I've misplaced a few things since we moved here. A necklace, my perfume, then there was this little teacup I swear had hot tea in it in the cottage when I first went down there to check it out. Later, I found it in our cupboard." She shakes her head. "I'm probably going insane," she tells me, smiling ruefully.

"I don't think that's it." I actually feel bad for her. At first, I did want to scare her. I wanted to scare both of them, to make them rethink ever moving here before I hurt Amy and got my revenge on Tim.

But now my goal has changed. I wanted to hurt Amy, sure, but now I see that I have to protect her. She reminds me so much of Wilma, and I just want to keep her safe. If I keep scaring her, then I'm not doing a good job of that. "I think moving is incredibly stressful, you're alone most of the day, which can be mentally taxing, and then you're under stress in your marriage."

She walks over to me and slumps into a chair by the table. "I don't want you to think Tim is a bad guy."

That's exactly what I think, but I don't say anything. I just wait until she's ready to talk again, and finally she does, the words spilling from her.

"He's not, really. He's under all this pressure at work, and then sometimes it comes out in how he interacts with people, but he's a great guy. He'd never do anything to hurt me on purpose. I just think this work trip was really ill-timed, but that's not his fault. That's Marie's."

"Marie?" I'm doing everything I can to keep Amy from realizing I know all this. I know who Marie is. She's not kind, always pushing her staff to make the hard decisions for her instead of making them herself, but still, I know how terrible her husband actually is. Tim didn't have to pick my folder. He didn't have to be the reason my wife is dead.

"His boss." She pushes herself up from the table. "She's out there, Paul." Amy turns her finger in a circle by the side of her head to get her point across. "On his first day at work she gave him folders of different employees and told him he had to fire one."

I freeze. "You mentioned this before. What did he do?" Does my voice sound normal? I don't want her to realize that I feel like I'm about to choke on the words as I speak them.

"He just grabbed one at random because he didn't know who to pick or how to choose the right person. He's felt bad about it since then." She goes to the counter and grabs a hammer and a nail from a drawer before pulling a picture off the wall by the window. "Will you please hang this up for me and cover the hole?"

I take the hammer, nail, and picture from her without thinking, then wait as she pushes the chair back for me so I can reach the hole. It only takes a few taps with the hammer to secure the nail, but I'm not thinking about what I'm doing.

I'm thinking about Tim.

He had me fired without even looking through the files? According to Amy, it honestly sounds like he didn't even bother to flip through them and try to make a good choice. He just took a dart, closed his eyes, threw it, and ruined my life.

And killed my wife.

I could kill his right now. She's watching me with so much trust and kindness in her eyes that I could choke it out of her and leave her here on the floor for Tim to find. My free hand clenches into a fist, and I have to force myself to relax it.

"Thanks for doing that." She reaches out for the hammer, and I have to force myself to give it to her. It would be so easy to bring it down on her temple and end this. But I don't. I don't want to. I love the way she looks at me, the sweet expression on her face, how kind she is.

I want to protect her. *I want to have her for my own.* It's the first time I've thought that, and I start, then push the thought aside to deal with later.

"Of course. Hopefully that gives you some peace of mind. I'll get out of your hair so you can get some sleep."

She smiles at me, but then her expression changes like she's just remembered something. "Oh! What did you need when you came back to the house? I'm so rude, I never even asked."

"Hmm," I say, still walking to the front door. "I don't remember, honestly. That feels like an hour ago."

She laughs. "I'm so sorry. If you remember, just let me know, okay? And have a good night, Paul. Thanks again for hanging up the picture."

"Of course." I'm halfway out the door, but I still turn to look at her. "Seriously, Amy, if you need anything, I'll help you. I really don't think there was someone in your walls, okay? If you get scared, just let me know. I'm right down the hill, and there's no way I'd let anything happen to you while your husband is gone."

The smile she gives me is small, but she trusts me. I know that she does.

She shouldn't.

24

TIM

B y the time Thursday rolls around, I'm more than ready to come home. I miss Amy, miss her cooking, and I certainly miss my bed. There's nothing like sleeping in your own bed when you've been on a terrible hotel mattress for days. In addition to all of that, I can't wait to see what Paul has gotten done around the house.

The way Amy talks, it sounds like the man is a miracle worker. I know she's been helping him a lot outside even though she's supposed to be spending as much time as possible writing her book now that we've hired him. As long as she gets her copywriting done for her clients, I guess it doesn't matter, but I know she doesn't want to write copy forever.

Susie wants to go out for dinner and karaoke again tonight, but I promised Amy that I would have a video-chat dinner with her instead. I know she's feeling left out by me being out with coworkers and having more fun than I'm letting on, but she's having a good time too, I'm sure of it.

And I know she's worried something will happen between me and Susie, but there's no way I'll ever make that mistake again. That was a onetime thing and something that the two of us barely came back from. Now that Amy and I are good again, there's just no way I'd risk losing her.

It's not me having an affair, physical or otherwise, that I'm really worried about.

I know she really likes Paul. He reminds her of what a father should be like, although hers wasn't ever around to look out for her. I'm not sure how healthy their relationship is, especially since we're paying him to do the yard work and she's always out there helping him, but it's not like I can tell her to stop.

Things are a little tenuous between the two of us.

There's a knock on my door, and I lean out, grabbing the Chinese food from the delivery man and tipping him heavily.

He grins at me and then scurries back down the hall.

See? I'm not a bad guy. I give good tips, and I take care of people. I know Amy doesn't like me being here, but I'm coming home soon. Besides, this trip was for my job, which means that it was for us. It wasn't like I wanted to leave her for a week.

After I'm settled in front of my computer, I pour myself a glass of wine. Firing up the video-chat app, I pause when my phone vibrates.

She'd better not miss dinner again.

Susie's name blinks on my screen with a single-word text.

Karaoke?

I frown. She already knows I have a little date planned with my wife but doesn't seem to care. Instead of responding, I turn my phone facedown on the desk and then look up right as Amy logs on.

She looks great, with her hair pulled back into a low

ponytail and just a bit of makeup on. For a moment, I drink her in, but before I can say anything, my phone rings.

"Sorry about that," I say, grabbing my phone and flipping it back over. It's Susie, and I silence the ringing before putting it back down. "Work stuff."

"At seven at night?" Amy arches an eyebrow at me. She has pizza in front of her and picks up a single slice. "You sure it wasn't your karaoke buddy wanting to know why you aren't out partying with her?" There's a bite to her words, but I do my best to ignore it.

This is not how I wanted this dinner with my wife to go, and I have to choke back any snarky remark I was going to make. Getting angry with Amy isn't going to solve anything and will only make her worry more about what's going on here.

"I want to be with you," I tell her, looking her right in the eyes. "Tell me what's been going on at home."

She pauses, pizza halfway to her mouth. "Nothing really. Doing lots of writing and helping Paul outside." Shrugging, she takes a bite.

Something's up. This is the first time we've video chatted since I got here, and even though we've texted a number of times, we haven't talked much on the phone. I can tell immediately that there's something going on that she doesn't want to share.

"What's bothering you?" I haven't even opened my dinner yet, and I'm not sure I want to. I need to find out what's going on with Amy, because it's obvious something's wrong.

She hesitates. "Okay, this is going to sound insane, Tim, but don't make fun of me." I nod, and she continues, "I think someone might be watching me."

"Watching you? What do you mean?"

"I know how it sounds, but I would have sworn someone

was watching me last night when I was in the kitchen. And I found a hole in the wall."

Now I have no idea what she's talking about. "You found a hole in the wall? Like, what, a mouse hole?"

"No." There's tension in her voice that wasn't there a moment ago, and I'm sure it's because she doesn't think I believe her. I do, I guess, it's just ...

It sounds insane.

"What kind of hole?"

"A hole. Like a peephole. It was up on the wall, and when I poked a wooden spoon into it, I couldn't feel anything, like there's a lot of space behind the wall."

There's no easy way for me to say what I'm about to say without pissing off my wife, but I have to do it. "You think someone was in the walls of the house watching you while you were ... what, cooking?"

"Yeah, cooking dinner." She's dropped her pizza back down on her plate and is staring at me like she's daring me to laugh at her.

"So you were all alone in the kitchen, making dinner. And you just felt someone's eyes on you?"

She nods.

"I have no idea what to say to you, Amy. There's absolutely no way someone was watching you. Don't you think we'd know if there was another person on the property?"

"Not if they were being sneaky." She leans forward, dropping her voice a little bit like she's afraid someone is going to hear her. "You think I'm nuts, don't you?"

"I don't. And why are you whispering? Do you think they're watching you right now? Maybe it's a ghost. Did Holly ever mention if anyone died in the house before we bought it?"

"A ghost? Really?" There's a flash of something in her eyes, like she was thinking this very thing and was afraid to mention it in case I made fun of her. "Come on, Tim. Don't joke with me like that unless you mean it. I ... I thought the same thing." She stares at me, her mouth falling open slightly, and I can easily see how worried she is. "Wait. You're making fun of me."

"I'm not."

My phone is on silent, but I see the screen light up with Susie's name. She's relentless, and I know I should be happier spending time with Amy right now, but I can't help but think that I'd be having a lot more fun if I were out drinking and singing.

"You know what? I knew I shouldn't mention it to you because you'd just think I'd lost the plot. This was stupid. I have no idea why we thought we should get together and share a meal over video chat. Besides, you want to be out drinking and partying, don't you?"

"I don't," I tell her, irritated that she can see right through me like that. "I want to be with you, Amy, and this is the best I can do right now, so—" Before I can defend myself further, though, there's banging on the door.

"Tiiiim! I know you're in there! It's our last night here, so let's go party!" Susie's voice is singsongy and carries right through the door.

I wince, sure that Amy can hear it.

"Nice, Tim. Really classy." Amy looks pissed, and I glance at the door, praying that Susie will stop banging on it.

"Amy, listen," I start, but before I can get another word out, her screen goes dark. "Dammit." Anger washes over me, and I grab the edge of my desk, trying to take deep enough breaths to calm down.

As I do, the banging on the door continues. "Come out and party!"

I shouldn't. I should call Amy back and tell her I'm sorry and that I believe her. I should get rid of Susie and tell her she has to leave me alone. I should call Holly and see if she knows anything about spaces in the walls or the possibility of ghosts. There are a million things I know I should be doing to make Amy feel better and keep her from being so angry at me, but I don't.

Instead, I grab my glass of wine and chug it as I walk across the room to throw open the door.

Susie stands there, looking triumphant. Her eyes are wide and her cheeks pink, and I know immediately that she's already been drinking.

"I thought you were just going to ignore me," she says, grinning up at me. "Let's go."

I shouldn't, but I do.

25

AMY

Tim comes back this afternoon, and I know I should be happy to see my husband after him being gone for so long, but I don't want him here right now. I can't stop wondering what's been going on between him and Susie, and I want him to figure out that he can't treat me the way he has been, and I want him to be nicer to me.

"Like that'll ever happen," I say to myself. I'm scrubbing the kitchen floor, which is something that probably needs to be done at least once a week judging by how messy a cook I am. There's sauce splattered here as well as some yolk from an egg. "A dog would take care of this," I say.

Turning my head, I look at the picture Paul hung up on the wall for me. He was so kind when I was scared and took care of the problem, unlike Tim, who just made fun of it and made me feel like I had lost my mind. The picture hangs there, looking a little out of place all by itself on the huge expanse of wall, but I had to have something there to keep me from feeling like I was being watched.

I know the hole is there, though, and even though it's

covered up, I still feel uncomfortable. What if there's more than one hole? I've been thinking that since I found it, and even though I know I should look for other places where someone could watch me, I'm terrified.

Suddenly I have to know if there are more holes in the walls.

I scurry through the house quickly, moving from room to room as quietly as possible. My ears hurt from straining them hard, listening for anyone moving through the house. So far, nothing, although I haven't gotten nearly as much sleep as I would like, so maybe I'm just a little off to begin with.

I keep waking up in the middle of the night with the uncanny feeling someone was in my room.

And don't get me started on the things I'm missing.

I'm moving slowly, taking my time as I work my way through every room in the house. I'm not sure what I'm hoping to find, just some proof that I'm not going insane, I guess.

Whatever it is, I don't find it and return to the kitchen. Running my hand along the kitchen counter, I turn and lean against it, staring at the picture on the wall.

I feel uncomfortable being in here, knowing the hole is there, but I need to finish the floor, then I can go somewhere else. Maybe my office or the garden to get some fresh air and try to clear my head.

Dropping to my knees, I squeeze out the rag in my bucket and then dunk it back in. I should get up and change out the dirty water for some clean water, but I'm so close to being done. It's not like Tim will spend a lot of time looking at the floor to see how clean it is.

The thought of my husband makes my back bristle. I'm just too frustrated at how he treated me this week to think about him right now, so I push any thought of him from my mind.

And that's when I hear the floorboards creak. I freeze, adrenaline making my muscles go cold, like I've just been dumped in a freezing cold swimming pool. I'm listening so hard I can hear my heart pounding in my ears.

There it is again.

It's coming from directly above me, like someone is walking down the hall upstairs. My fingers are clamped tightly around the wet rag, and I can't make myself let go, but I turn my head slowly, looking up at the ceiling.

Another creak and a shiver runs up my spine.

What the hell do I do?

Slowly I stand, forcing myself to let go of the rag. It falls to the ground with a soft squelch, but I can't tear my eyes from the ceiling. I don't see anything. There's nothing to see.

But it sounds like footsteps. I'd swear on my mother's grave there's someone walking around up there.

Fumbling in my pocket, I look for my phone, but it's not there. When I close my eyes, I see it plugged in to charge upstairs by my computer. I hadn't wanted to bring it with me because I honestly didn't care if Tim reached out to me. I was being childish, and now that's come back to bite me in the butt.

I could run. I could flee the house and look for Paul and tell him I'm scared. He'd drop everything and come to help me, I just know it, but by then whoever is upstairs could be long gone.

No, I have to go up there. I'm terrified of doing that, but I don't think I have a choice if I want to prove to Tim that I haven't lost my mind. The footsteps have stopped, so I hurry to the knife block by the stove and grab a knife, weighing it in my hand.

Sure, I've seen the news reports that say you're actually really likely to be killed by your own weapon if you don't know what you're doing, but I can't force myself to go upstairs without something to protect myself. The handle is smooth, and I grip it tightly, jabbing it into the air in front of me a few times to get a feel for it.

It'll have to do.

Hurrying to the stairs, I grab the banister and take a deep breath.

There it is again. I hear a footstep, then another, like someone is moving faster now through the house. I'm not insane, I know what I'm hearing, and I have to figure out what I'm going to do about it.

My heart beats in my throat as I take the first step, then another. My entire body feels like it's on fire, like my nerves are all screaming for me to stop this nonsense and run and find Paul instead, but I have to know the truth. I have to know if someone is up there, and find out what they want.

I'm racing up the stairs, no longer worried about being quiet. If someone is in my house, then I'm going to find them, and I'm going to stop them. Tim will have a lot to apologize for then.

Reaching the landing, I pause, listening. The footsteps have stopped, but I turn towards my office. This is where I thought I heard the footsteps first, before they were right above me, and I'm hoping it's where I'll find proof that someone was in my house.

I take each step carefully, slowly putting my foot down, slowly shifting my weight. My heart slams hard, and I feel light-headed, but I reach out to the wall with one hand for support as I inch carefully towards my office.

The door is ajar. Did I leave it like that? I can't remember. All I remember is leaving my phone there, looking out the window once at the still garden, then heading downstairs. I hadn't wanted to write copy today, but if I'd stayed at my computer, then the chances are good I might have come face-to-face with whoever was making the noises.

At the door I hesitate before reaching out and carefully pushing it open. It swings open silently, and I hold my breath, searching the space for someone.

I see my desk with my laptop. There's a stack of books on the floor where Tim keeps promising me he'll get me a bookshelf. The window doesn't have any curtains because I want to be able to enjoy an unobstructed view.

That's it. My chair is right where I left it, turned slightly away from the desk when I got up to go downstairs, but I don't see anything out of place.

I listen, closing my eyes to block out any distraction as I try to pick up on any squeaking or footsteps. I'm sure I wasn't hearing things, making stuff up.

But there's nothing.

My body sags a little as I lean against the doorframe. I need to check out the rest of the second floor, I'm sure of that. First, though, I'll get my phone just in case I have to make a call. I hurry across my office and grab the phone from where I left it charging. It's full, and I see that I have a message from Tim, but I don't bother reading it now.

He's coming home today, and it's probably just him telling me how excited he is to come home and how much he can't wait to see me.

My eyes flick across my desk as I slip my phone into my pocket. My laptop is there, as is my notebook where I jot down ideas for the book I've been working on. My favorite pen is right on top of it, but something's not right.

Laptop. Notebook. Pen. Phone. Water cup. Frame.

My eyes fall on the ornate metal frame Tim bought me after we got married so I could display a wedding picture on my desk. I've always hated that frame, always thought it was over the top and ostentatious. I would have been much happier with a simple wooden frame, but Tim thought it was gorgeous and told me that it would mean a lot to him if I used it.

So I did.

The frame is there, all twisted metal with a shiny pane of glass.

But our wedding photo is gone.

26

PAUL

That was close. I hurry down to my little room where I keep my Amy mementos and only stop to catch my breath when I'm in there and have laid the picture on the table.

Amy moved faster than I thought she would. I never imagined she would get a kitchen knife and come looking through the house to see what was making the noise upstairs. I didn't want to scare her, but I hadn't had a lot of time to explore her office on my own. I needed some alone time in there to feel like I was getting to know her better.

But she heard me and came flying up the stairs.

Picking up the photo I stole, I trace my finger down her face. She's so gorgeous, and in this picture she looks so happy and trusting. If she'd known then what a monster Tim was, would she have ever walked down the aisle to marry him? I don't think she would have. She's too kind, too loving.

He doesn't deserve her.

Picking up a nail from the floor, I use it to scratch out Tim's face. He looks happy in the picture, too happy, and I hate seeing him next to Amy when I know who he really is.

Satisfied, I put the photo down, then pick it up again, weighing it in my hand. It doesn't weigh anything, but I feel the heaviness of what it means for me.

Tim's face is obliterated, but I can still see Amy. I'm doing her a favor, getting rid of him. I just wish she could see that and understand it. Maybe if she knew how terrible he was, she would get it. If she knew he was the reason my Wilma was dead, she might even want to help me.

But it's better not to risk it. I'll just handle everything on my own. That's the best way I can make sure that this is all taken care of.

Carefully, I slip Wilma's picture from the frame and set it on the table. "I love you. You'd like her, I promise you. She's so much like you," I tell her, stroking the picture before replacing it with Amy's. She's striking, and though it's weird to see her face there instead of my wife's, it's not a bad thing.

I go back outside, whistling to myself. The day is shaping up to be a gorgeous one. Tim will be home soon, but I'm actually really excited about that. Once he's home, I can take care of this. He doesn't deserve Amy.

All of this is for her.

Walking slowly through the front garden, I glance up at the house. I already know I can't easily see into Amy's office window, but if she's looking outside, then she'll see me. Sure enough, before I'm past the front porch, she steps out, waving her arm above her head to get my attention.

"Paul! Do you have a moment?" Her voice is clear and strong, but I detect a slight waver of fear. Amy is scared, and while that's no longer my intention, I do want her to know that she can turn to me for help.

I change direction immediately. "What's going on, Amy? You okay?"

She looks spooked and shakes her head, biting her lower

lip. "You know how I found the hole in my kitchen wall yesterday?"

I nod. She hasn't found more, I know that. I've been keeping an extra close eye on her since then, and I haven't gotten much sleep at all. It's comforting to enter her bedroom at night to make sure she's okay.

"Someone was upstairs in the house just now." She drops her voice and rubs her arms like she's cold. "I know it sounds crazy, but I promise you, I heard someone up there."

"In the house?" Scratching my chin, I look up at the building. "How would they have gotten in?"

She shrugs. "That's the thing. I've been keeping the doors locked all the time now. Even when I'm out here with you, I lock them and bring my key with me." She looks a little embarrassed by this. "I think I'm losing my mind, Paul."

Oh, Amy. I don't want her to think that. I don't want her to feel like she's going insane. She's so sweet and innocent, and it really isn't her fault any of this is happening. "You're not going crazy," I assure her. "If you think you heard something, then you probably did, but I have no idea how a person could have gotten into your house. Do you want me to come look through it with you?"

She hesitates, and I know she's embarrassed to ask, but that's exactly what she wants. Finally, she gives a little nod. "Do you mind?"

"Of course not. If my Wilma was scared and someone didn't take time out of their day to make sure she was safe, then I'd be incredibly upset." I hesitate, already knowing the answer to my next question, but wanting to make it seem like I don't. "Have you talked to Tim about this?"

Her face darkens slightly, and she gives her head a quick shake. "He's not taking me seriously right now. I talked to him about the hole in the kitchen wall, but he doesn't think it's a big deal." She pauses, tapping her chin with her finger.

"Maybe if you talked to him, he might realize this is serious. Would you be willing to do that?"

This is unexpected, and I'm immediately curious as to how I can work this for my own benefit. "If you want me to talk to him, of course I will," I say, speaking slowly so I can carefully choose my words. "But not until he's settled in this weekend. I think you should definitely try talking to him first. I don't want to get involved in something between the two of you and cause a problem."

She flushes. "You're right, I'm sorry, I shouldn't have asked. It's just—"

"I didn't say I wouldn't help you," I tell her gently, putting my hand on her lower back to turn her and guide her up to the house. "All I said was I thought that you and Tim should talk about it first so he has the chance to take you seriously. I'm sure if he knew how much he was hurting you, he would want to change his behavior."

She's silent as we go into the house. Hesitating at the bottom of the stairs, she points up them. "Do you mind? I was in the kitchen, and I'm sure I heard someone upstairs."

She's right, she did. I just had to get in her office and poke around up there. I wanted to be moving around in the house when she was awake to see how it felt. It's one thing being in the house while she's sleeping and to keep an eye on her, but I wanted to be there while she was awake.

"Lead the way."

She gives me a shy smile and hurries up the stairs.

I take my time, enjoying following her up to the second floor. This is what it could be like if Tim wasn't here. I didn't think I wanted to have a relationship with Amy, not like that, but I was wrong. I want to be there for her and protect her. It feels really good to know that I'm there for her now, that she can turn to me, that she trusts me.

Amy needs me. She's so gentle, so fragile. Just like my Wilma.

"You know my office," she says, leading me into the space. "I'm pretty sure the footsteps came from up here. And, okay, I know this sounds crazy, but our wedding photo is gone."

"A photo?" I ask, glancing around the room. She doesn't know where to look in the gaudy wallpaper to see the hole drilled in the wall so I can watch her while she works. She doesn't see the way part of the wainscoting forms a door that can easily be pulled out of the way for me to come and go. Her eyes aren't trained for this sort of thing, and that's what I love about her.

She's just so innocent.

"I know it seems impossible, and that's what Tim would say." Amy sounds bolder now since I haven't dismissed her concerns, and she walks over to the desk, picks up the gaudiest picture frame I've ever seen, and hands it to me. "See? This place is weird." I take it from her, and she crosses her arms on her chest. "Don't get me wrong, I love the house and the gardens, and what you're doing to them is amazing, but I get a weird feeling here."

"Because you think you're being watched?" I'm calm as I can be on the outside, but internally I feel giddy, like a little kid. Never did I imagine Amy would pick up on what was going on around here. Never did I think she was that smart. Sweet? Yes. In need of someone to protect her? Definitely. But I didn't think she'd come close to figuring anything out.

"Yes. And because I think someone or something is messing with me. The hot cup of tea," she says, ticking things off on her fingers, "the way things have gone missing, the feeling of being watched, and now the footsteps. It's all too much. I want to know more about this house." She gives herself a little nod like she's just decided to do something she should have done a while ago. "I'm going to call the Realtor and ask her what else she knows."

My blood runs cold. Surely Holly won't slip up and give her any information. We bought a phone just for this purpose, so she could pretend to be a Realtor, but I still don't want her to mess up.

But then the more I think about it, the more I realize this is a better way forward. If Amy were to look online, she would easily find out whom the house belonged to before. She might even put two and two together.

She might find out the house used to be mine.

"I think that's a fine idea," I tell her, putting a smile on my face. "She might be able to put all your fears to rest. Maybe you have a resident ghost, and you are just going to have to learn to live with them. Or an angel, like I said, remember? Come on, we'll look around the rest of the second floor just to be sure."

"A ghost? Maybe." She doesn't sound convinced and hasn't moved to leave the office to continue our search. "But I think there's more going on here than just a ghost. I think someone is messing with me, but I don't know why. I'll find out, though."

As I stare at her, I have a horrible thought. I keep thinking Tim is the one I have to get rid of.

But what if Amy catches on to me before I get rid of Tim and have a chance to show her how happy she can be with me?

27

TIM

The entire drive home I'm worried about what I'm going to say to my wife when I see her. This week wasn't supposed to be an incredible vacation, but even if I did hope to enjoy myself from time to time, she made sure I couldn't.

It's terrible of me to feel that way about her, but it was obvious from the moment I left and started having fun with some of the people attending the leadership classes that Amy wasn't happy with what I was doing. She hated the fact I wasn't sitting in my hotel room all alone every single night, and I can't help but admit that I hate the fact she was hanging out with someone else all the while.

I didn't have an affair, but did she ... no, the thought is too terrible for me to even consider, and I push it out of my mind.

It doesn't matter that the person she spent so much time with is old enough to be her father or that I know, deep in my heart, Amy wouldn't ever do anything to hurt me. The fact remains I was in classes all day learning how to be better at my job so I can make sure I'm providing for our little family while she was hanging out with Paul, probably not working

nearly as much as she was supposed to, and getting homemade meals every single night.

My hand tightens on the steering wheel. It's probably
silly to be so upset with her, but I can't help it. I hate the
thought of Amy having fun without me, and I know as soon
as I'm home and we settle back into our routine, any bad
feelings the two of us harbored while I was away will
disappear.

She'll know I was faithful to her, and I can make sure she
and Paul aren't up to anything.

That's just how our relationship works. We might get
frustrated with each other from time to time, but I wouldn't
ever do anything to hurt her again, and I certainly wouldn't
wish her harm. The problem is, I haven't been home to keep
an eye on things and make sure the two of us are on a good
footing.

My car eats up the miles home, and I press down on the
gas a little harder, hoping I'll be able to make good time. Amy
and I haven't spoken today, although I did send her a text to
let her know I was on my way. I don't want her to think I was
still upset with her, even though I am pretty irritated with her
right now.

That doesn't mean we won't have things smoothed over
by the time I go back to work on Monday. And I'm sure my
wife will be happy when I tell her I won't be seeing Susie
again. There isn't any threat there, no problem that our
marriage can't overcome, and I'm determined to make sure
we're on a solid footing again as soon as possible.

I'm about an hour away from home, taking the turns as
quickly as I can, when my phone rings. I can't help the jolt of
excitement that shoots through me when I see Amy's name
on the screen. Grinning to myself, I tap on the screen and
send her voice through my car's speakers.

"Hey, honey," I say, keeping my voice light and happy like

we haven't been at each other's throats all week long. "How are you doing? I can't wait to see you."

"Tim, hi," she says, sounding a little distracted. "Are you still coming home for dinner tonight?"

I chuckle a little nervously. "Of course I am, that's been the plan the entire time. Why do you have a question about it now?"

"Oh, just checking." There's a pause, and I hear someone speaking to her, but they're not loud enough for me to make out what they're saying or who it is.

That's okay, I don't need to hear the person's voice to know exactly whom my wife is talking to.

Paul.

I know it just like I know my name. He's in the house with her right now, or she's in his little cottage, or they're meeting in the garden. It doesn't matter to me where they are talking, what matters is the fact that I want my wife's full attention right now, and I don't get to have it because of the caretaker.

"Are you talking to Paul?" I can't help the words that burst from my mouth. "Were you two coming up with dinner plans, and I'm just interrupting them?"

"What? No." Amy sighs. "I mean, yes, I was talking to him, but it's not like he and I had some big plans you weren't privy to, Tim. I'm not the one going out every single night with strange women my spouse doesn't know."

So this is how it's going to be? A few days away from my wife, all I want to do is go home to her, and she's going to act like she's not even happy to see me? I didn't do anything wrong, I certainly didn't cheat on her, yet Amy's acting like I'm some horrible person she can't believe she got suckered into marrying.

"Do you mind if we talk privately?" I have to fight to keep the frustration out of my voice, but I know getting angry with her isn't going to solve anything. All it will do is make her mad, and she'll hang up the phone, leaving me to wonder exactly what she's doing.

"We are talking privately." Her words are clipped. "But since you seem so worried about someone listening in, I'll go outside."

So he was in the house with her.

I wait a moment for her to go outside, and when I hear the slam of the screen door, I speak again. "Listen, Amy, I think this week has been harder on the two of us than it needed to be. I'm sorry I upset you just now, and I want you to know I'm really excited to see you again."

She pauses, and I can practically feel her weighing her options. "You weren't here for me this week, and I needed you."

What is she talking about? "I'm sorry, Amy, but I'm here now, and I'll be physically with you really soon. Talk to me. What's been going on?"

Another sigh. "Tim, it's been really weird since we moved in, but you haven't seemed to notice, and you don't seem to care."

That's a low blow, but I ignore it.

"I've been scared here a lot. First the teacup, which I know you don't believe actually happened, so you don't need to remind me, then things missing from our room. I don't like it, Tim. I really think the place is haunted."

"Haunted? Honey, I was kidding about the ghost. You didn't think I was serious, did you?" I leave for a week, and my wife goes completely off the deep end. I swear, if Paul has been putting these thoughts in her head, then I will have to have some words with him. I'm sure we can find another caretaker who isn't as prone to meddling in our marriage if that's what it all comes down to.

"Or someone is watching me. I found a peephole in the

kitchen wall, Tim. Someone was there, watching me. They were in the walls. I'm serious."

I shake my head. "Amy, I think you're just nervous because you've been by yourself in the house for so long. There's absolutely no way anyone was in the walls. First of all, how would they get in? How would they survive? They'd have to have food and water and a bathroom ..." I let my voice trail off to see if she's going to pick up on what I'm saying.

I love Amy. I know she's scared, and I hate that for her, but this is just ridiculous. There's absolutely no proof of anyone living in the walls of our house except for the fact that she has an uncomfortable feeling about something, and that's not enough to prove a damn thing.

"I knew you wouldn't believe me." Her voice is flat, and there's a current of anger running through it. "I told Paul you weren't going to believe me."

Paul again. "Does Paul think someone might be living in the walls? Is he the one putting these thoughts in your head?" I'm angry now, and I drive faster, completely ignoring the speed limit. I'm close enough to home that I'm pretty sure I can make it without running into problems, and I'm willing to take that risk.

"He talks me through it instead of shutting me down like you do!"

So much for people not listening in to our conversation. I wince as her words cut through the air to me. "Then thank God you have Paul there to help you," I snap. I'm flying past cars now, dominating the left lane of the interstate. My exit is coming up soon, but then I have to take the back roads all the way to our house, and it would be dangerous to drive this fast on them.

She hangs up without saying another word.

"Dammit!" I yell, slamming my hand into the steering wheel. I don't know what the hell kind of game Paul is playing at the house with my wife, but I do know I need to get there as soon as possible.

Signaling, I move over to the right lane so I won't blow past my exit.

And then the blue lights fill my car.

28

PAUL

I wait until Amy comes back in from the porch after talking to Tim. She looks exhausted and has bright spots of color in her cheeks, but when I raise my eyebrows at her in question, she just flaps her hand at me and motions for me to follow her to the kitchen.

Of course, I heard it all. She wasn't exactly quiet, and I already know Tim isn't my biggest fan. I know he thinks that Amy is crazy for being worried about living in the house, and that's all my fault.

"Everything okay?" I ask as Amy drags a kitchen stool over to the refrigerator. There are cupboards above it on the wall, and she opens one, leaning as far forward as she can before handing down a bottle of whiskey.

"I want a drink," she tells me, taking the hand I offer to help her down. "That's Tim's special whiskey that he only drinks when he has something to celebrate, but I don't care right now. I want something to drink, and it's the only thing we have in the house."

Wiping some dust from the top of the bottle, I unscrew it

and wait while Amy gets glasses. I pour us each a measure and take a sip of mine while she tosses hers back.

"More." She holds her glass out to me, and I pour in more whiskey. After she downs that, I fill it once more; then she finally motions for us to sit at the table. "Okay, that's good. Do you like it?"

I take another small sip to be polite. I've never been a big drinker, and I don't intend on starting now, but I'm not going to leave Amy drinking alone. "It's delicious."

"He knows how to choose his whiskey," Amy says, spinning her glass on the table. After a moment of silence, she looks up at me. "He doesn't believe a word I said."

"About what?" She can't know I heard her side of the conversation or that it made me giddy. I want to hurt Tim, and if Amy has already mentally moved on from her husband, then she won't be hurt, as well.

"That this place is creepy," she says, waving a hand in the air. "That I feel nervous here, that I think someone was watching me. I didn't tell him about all the things that are missing, but I don't think he'd get it, anyway. He doesn't care, and that scares me."

I nod. I don't even have to pretend to look like I care. I'm honestly worried about Amy, and I want her to be okay. "Do you want me around when he gets home, just to act as a buffer?"

She shrugs, then looks up at me. "Yes and no. I want you here because you make me feel safe when you're in the house with me, but I don't think you being around will make Tim happy. He already feels a little weird not being home this week and not being around when I needed him."

"The last thing I want to do is cause friction between the two of you. When he gets home, I'll just make myself scarce and go down to my cottage, okay?"

"Thank you." She has tears shining in her eyes and

reaches across the table to give my hand a squeeze. "I don't know what I'd do without you here. You're ... well, I know it sounds crazy, but it feels like you're my guardian angel. Don't laugh," she says when I smile. "I really love having you around and can't imagine what I would have done this week without you here."

"It was my pleasure, believe me." I squeeze her fingers and then let go. "Now, let's talk about something a bit happier, okay? What are you looking forward to doing this weekend?"

Her face lights up, just like I knew it would. She's been spending a lot of time working on her book, when she would normally be writing copy. I've watched through the hole in her office wall while she downed cups of coffee one after another, coaxing the words from her mind and carefully putting them on paper.

She hasn't let me read it yet, but I know how excited she is. I saw her celebrate last night with a glass of wine before she printed off the entire manuscript. She left it on her desk with the empty wine bottle when she went to bed, and I snuck out from the wall to read part of it.

It's good. Better than I would have thought, which makes me proud of her. I want her to be successful, and if success to her means being an author, then I hope she can get an agent for her book. She left a red pen on top of the manuscript, and I had to resist the urge to mark it up for her.

That was what I would have done before, but not now.

I want to support her now, not scare her.

"Okay, I haven't told anyone this, but I finished my book." She grins at me, giving a little wiggle of excitement in her chair.

I smack my hand on the table in surprise. "Congratulations! That's huge! Tell me everything about it!"

"Really? You want to know about the book? I kinda thought you said that just to be nice."

I nod. I didn't read far enough to see how the hero was going to handle the conflict she set up for him, and I want to know what she's going to do. Besides, I have a very good feeling Tim isn't going to care one bit about a book his wife has written. Someone needs to be excited for her, and I'm more than happy to be that person.

"It's a middle-grade portal fantasy," she tells me, her fingers tracing the top of her glass. "And the hero, Mike, has to get through the portal that appears only once a year in the forest behind his house because he believes someone came through that portal years ago and kidnapped his sister."

I listen with interest as she works her way through the book, telling me all the things Mike is going to have to do to save his sister. We're close to the end of the book when suddenly headlights sweep across the front windows.

Amy freezes. "It's Tim," she whispers.

I nod, pushing back from the table as quickly as possible. "I'll go out the back," I tell her. "Follow me and lock it so you don't have to worry about it later."

We hurry through the house, and I throw open the lock on the back door before slipping out. It's dark out, the moon just beginning to crest the trees, and Amy turns on the outside light so I can see.

"Turn it off," I whisper. "I'm fine in the dark. I know my way around better than you'd think."

As soon as the words are out of my mouth, I wish I could take them back, but if Amy thinks they're odd, she doesn't let on. Relief floods through my body when she gives me a quick nod and flicks the light off. We're both bathed in the dark, and even though it's hard to see right now, I know I'll be just fine as soon as my eyes adjust in a few minutes.

"Good luck," I whisper, stepping away from the house. I'm

not headed down to my cottage, even though I'm sure that's where she thinks I'm going. I have to get under the house and then make my way up into the walls so I can keep an eye on what's going on. I want to make sure Amy is safe and Tim doesn't get too angry with her.

I have to protect her.

29

AMY

The last time I was this nervous to see Tim was on our wedding day, and my heart hurts. It's pounding so hard as I lock the back door and run through the house to the kitchen. I make it there right as Tim walks through the front door. He drops his suitcase on the floor and tosses his jacket on the table before he turns to look at me, frustration and exhaustion written all over his face.

Maybe he wouldn't be so tired if he hadn't spent all week partying every night.

I wish I could say that to him, but I'm afraid to, and instead I give him a huge smile. "Welcome home, Tim. I missed you."

He nods at me, then glances past me into the kitchen. Turning to see what he's looking at, I feel my stomach sink when I see the two glasses out on the kitchen table. I completely forgot to put one of them away, and I'm sure he'll know that Paul was in the house with me.

"Who were you drinking with?" he asks, walking over to the table and picking up Paul's glass. It's still mostly full, and

Tim swirls the amber liquid around inside it. "And why did you crack open the good whiskey without me?"

"I was just waiting on you," I say, eyeballing Paul's glass in my husband's hand. It's probably stupid to lie to him, but I have a very good feeling Tim will only get really angry if he knows Paul was here. It's stupid that he would act like that when I just want a friend, but it's not worth the fight.

"That's sweet of you." He downs the whiskey and sets the glass down hard on the table.

"Did something happen on the drive home?" Tim doesn't usually sound this angry, but I can tell something is bothering him. His eyes keep flicking around the kitchen like he's looking for proof I've done something bad or am lying to him. He seems on edge, and I don't like it.

"I got a speeding ticket after I talked to you." Finally, he turns and looks at me, and I almost wish he hadn't. "I was pretty upset when we got off the phone."

"I'm so sorry," I tell him. "Was the ticket bad?"

"Bad enough." He shrugs. "But I'll take care of it. I want to know what it is that has you so spooked right now. You look like you've seen a ghost."

I shake my head, plastering a smile on my face. "Sorry, it's just been a really long week, and I'm glad to have you home." It hits me that I haven't hugged him since he got into the house, so I walk to him, putting my arms around him and squeezing. "I missed you."

"I missed you, too." He rubs my back and then pulls away from me. "I'm sorry I was dismissive earlier. Tell me everything. What other weird things have been going on here?"

Is he serious? It feels as though he cares, unlike when he was away. Now that he's home, maybe that's all in the past. I hope it is, because I want my husband back.

"You said that things were going missing?" he prompts.

"Yes. There's a photo that's gone. Just ... out of the frame,"

I tell him, sure he won't be able to argue that I simply misplaced it. It's one thing for my perfume to go missing and Tim brushing it off and telling me I don't remember where I left it, but for a photo in a frame to go missing is something else entirely. "Come up to my office, okay?"

He follows me, and I'm actually nervous as I flick on the light and point to my desk. "The wedding photo I keep in that frame has gone. The frame is there, but the photo is missing."

"Okay. When was the last time you were in here today?" He crosses the room to my desk.

I lean against the doorframe to wait, watching him. "Um, a few hours ago while cleaning the house. That's when I saw it. I had to pop upstairs for a moment, and it was gone." Relief washes over me as I watch Tim. Even though it's been a really rough week for the two of us, I can't help but think that maybe it's all finally drawn to a close. Tim and I are strong, and everything is going to be fine.

He'll figure out what's going on, and now that he's back, hopefully Susie is out of his life. That means I'm not going to have to worry about him doing something stupid. With Tim here now, it almost seems like all the worry I had this week was over nothing.

"Amy." Tim's voice has a hard edge to it, and when he turns around to look at me, he's holding the picture frame. "Is this some kind of joke?"

"That's what I thought at first," I tell him, walking across the room to meet him. "I had no idea where the picture could have gone, though. And who would want it? That's why I kinda think we have a ghost." I chuckle to lighten the mood, because the dark look etched on Tim's face is anything but light and pleasant.

"Not funny, Amy. You actually had me thinking something might be wrong, and then this is what I come home to?"

He turns the frame around for me to see, and I take a step back.

The photo is back in the frame.

Kinda.

Well, a *different* photo of the two of us.

It's also from our wedding, but this one was in a frame in our bedroom. Tim's face is scratched out. His body is still visible. I can see my hand on his chest, and I'm grinning at the camera, but Tim's face has been destroyed. I look from the photo up to my husband, who is silently staring at me.

"What the hell is this?" Tim sounds pissed. His words are like nails on a chalkboard. His eyebrows are furrowed, and his mouth is set in a firm, straight line, a sure sign he's not going to back down from this conversation until he gets the answers he wants.

"I don't know," I say, and I really don't. "I swear to you, I don't know why it's like that."

"You said it was missing," he says, shoving the picture into my face like I can't already see it where it is. "You said it was missing. I wanted to be compassionate and believe you, but this is what you wanted me to see? Did you do this to punish me for having fun while I was in Raleigh?"

His nostrils flare, and his eyes narrow a little as he stares at me. I know he's pissed, and I take a step back before I answer him.

"No," I finally say, shaking my head. "I didn't do it, I promise you! I have no idea where the other photo went or why there's a different one here now, but I didn't take it out and do that." I point at the picture, and my hand shakes. "You really think I would do that to ... what, to *punish* you? Do you need punishing?"

"I think you're upset that I was having fun in Raleigh and you were alone here with Paul, so you latched onto him to make yourself feel better. Pathetic." Turning, he slams the picture frame down on my desk. It tips over and falls flat, but he doesn't move to pick it up. "You just couldn't stand me having a good time without you, could you?"

"Will you listen to yourself!" I scream the words at him; my hands ball into fists at my sides. "Do you hear what you're saying? You honestly think I would scratch out your face and then bring you up here to show you? What would I gain from doing that?"

"Maybe you just wanted to make me feel bad," he accuses. "And if you didn't do it, then who the hell did? Do you think a stranger just ... what, snuck in here while you were out or sleeping or something and scratched it out? Tell me, Amy, what theory do you have that would actually make sense?"

I have no idea, and I shake my head, backing away from him further. "I don't know," I mutter. "I kept all the doors and windows locked. Nobody has been in this house."

"Except for you and Paul."

"What?" I stare at him, trying to decide if he's really implying what I think he is.

"You said you two were the only ones in the house and that you didn't ruin the photo. That leaves one person who could have done it. Paul." Tim actually looks proud of himself, like he's just figured out a difficult puzzle.

"No, you're wrong. There's no way Paul would do something like this. And how? It's not like I let him into the house and then went off to read or anything. I was here the entire time he was."

"It was him, I know it. You let him in to get back at me. You got close to him to try to hurt me, and what happened? He took it as an excuse to try to drive a wedge between us."

"No." Tim's wrong. He has to be wrong. Paul was the only person who made me feel safe and secure this week. He wouldn't do something like that, wouldn't want to hurt me.

But if Tim hears me, he doesn't respond. Instead, he

pushes past me, roughly bumping me out of the way with his shoulder in his hurry to get out the door.

"Tim, no!" I cry, turning after him. "You've got it all wrong, you know you do! You just don't want to admit it!"

He doesn't answer, and I don't know how to stop him as he stomps down the hall.

30

PAUL

I see Tim turn away from Amy, see the bright red of his cheeks and the thunderstorms in his eyes. It's obvious just how angry he is, and I'm only grateful his anger is directed at me and not at his sweet wife.

If Amy were to be the brunt of his anger, then I'd feel terrible about what I'm doing, but it doesn't seem like he's mad at her.

He's coming for me.

Adrenaline courses through my veins, and I turn, running through the walls, no longer afraid of making noise. I'd crept up here as quietly as I possibly could before Tim followed Amy up the stairs to her office. I'd wanted to make sure they didn't hear me when I placed the new photo in the frame, but now it doesn't matter.

My heart slams so hard I can hear the beat in my ears like we're at the beach and the roaring of the waves has taken over all my senses. I have to turn to the side to shimmy around the corner, then I hurry on again, but I know I'm behind Tim.

He's going to leave the house, and I know where he's heading.

The cottage.

My heart pounds as I work my way down the makeshift ladder I made to help me move between floors. It's just a number of pieces of two by four hammered into the wall, and my toe slips once on my way down. Swearing softly to myself, I catch the tips of my fingers on the rung I almost missed and manage to pull myself back up.

Sweat beads on my forehead, and I reach up, wiping it away.

I'm scared, but also excited.

This is what I've been working towards. Everything I'm doing right now is to save Amy from her marriage to Tim. I want to protect her and make sure he can't ever hurt her the way he hurt me.

The way he hurt Wilma.

I'm out of breath by the time my feet hit the floor in the basement, but I still take time to make sure the trapdoor above me is shut. It leads straight up into the space behind the walls, making it easier for me to move around freely, and I don't want anyone else to find it. Unless you know what you're looking for, chances are good you won't see it.

Satisfied that everything looks as normal as possible, I wipe my hands on my pants and then bend over, taking a few deep breaths. Everything with Tim is about to come to a head, and I need to be as calm as I can. The last thing I want is for him to take one look at me and know something's up.

When I'm as calm as I can make myself, I turn and walk outside, glancing out the door leading into the garden first to make sure nobody is there waiting for me. From here, I can see the light on in my cottage. It's quiet out, the wind blowing softly through the garden, and I pause, listening for any signs of where Tim might be before pulling the door behind me.

He's angry, and I don't want to run into him until I'm prepared.

I knew I would get to this point with the man who killed my wife, but I didn't think it would happen so quickly. Cutting around the side of the house, I work my way down through the garden, keeping one eye on the cottage to spot Tim, but also glancing back over my shoulder from time to time to make sure he hasn't snuck up behind me.

"Tim!" Amy's voice cuts through the night. She sounds terrified and stressed, and I feel bad that this is how her night is going to go, but I have to end this. I need to protect her, and I need to get justice for my sweet wife, who didn't deserve to die. "Tim, where are you?"

"Where are you, Tim?" I ask, keeping my voice nice and low. I can move quickly through the garden without making much noise even though I'm not on the path.

Where others might crunch and snap twigs and dead plants I still need to clean up, I'm quiet as I move closer and closer to the cottage.

It's incredibly still by my cottage, but I'm not stupid enough to rush into it. He could be waiting for me there. Pausing, I lower myself down to the ground, my ears painful from straining to listen.

Nothing.

"Where the hell are you, Tim?" I keep my voice low and slowly turn and look over my shoulder. Thanks to the moon I can see the garden, but there are long shadows and strange shapes that make it difficult to tell what is what in the dark. Nothing moves, and I look back at the cottage.

He's not there.

Or he's waiting on me.

I wipe my hands on my jeans to dry them and pull a pair of small clippers from my pocket. They won't offer the best protection if I run into him in the dark, but any real weapon I would have used is either in my cottage or in the shed up by the house, and I'm not going to hurry all the way back up there to get something.

Not when I might be able to end this right now.

Still crouching, I move forward, my thighs screaming as I work my way through the brush. I'm still quiet, and I pause every few steps just to make sure there isn't any movement coming towards me that I might miss.

Rather than breathing through my nose, I suck little gasps in through my mouth. I have to stay quiet, have to keep my head down, have to find Tim before he finds me.

There's a small patch of grass around my cottage I'm going to have to walk across to get to the front door. Now I hover uncertainly in the underbrush of the garden, waiting to see if I can see Tim before I move.

He's not here.

It doesn't make any sense to me, but when I move closer, when I dare to cut across the grass and look in the window, my cottage is empty. Swearing, I stand and hurry to the door, throwing it open and stepping inside.

He's not here, and I don't know if he ever was.

The cottage is slightly cool from the open window, and nothing looks out of place. I'm about to look for a better weapon to defend myself against Tim when I run into him when I hear a scream.

Amy.

31

TIM

Amy's scream cuts through the night, and I know I should be mad at her for drawing attention to us, but maybe her cry will draw Paul out of hiding so I can finish this tonight.

"Where is he? I know you know. I know you two have been up to something. You've been with him every single night." I brandish the clippers I found in the toolshed at my wife. They're old and rusted, and I vaguely remember telling Paul he could buy whatever new tools he wanted and we would pay for them, but it's obvious he didn't replace these yet.

No matter. All I want to do is protect my wife, and I know what I have to do to keep her safe and prove to her how much I love her, even if that means scaring her first. She doubted my love and commitment while I was in Raleigh and spending time with Susie, I just know it, but now's my chance to fix that.

"What's wrong with you?" Amy's eyes are wide, and she takes a step back from me.

She came off the porch to see what was happening. I

want to ask her who she was looking for, me or Paul, but the reality is that maybe I don't want to know. If she was looking for Paul to protect him, then I don't know what I'll do.

"I'm protecting you!" I scream at her. "You were so upset the entire time I was gone, and now I'm going to show you how much you matter to me!"

"Not like this," she says, gesturing at the clippers I'm holding. "What are you planning on doing, Tim, killing him?"

"Is that what you want me to do?" I take a step closer to her, barely registering that she moves away from me. "Do you want me to kill him to keep you safe? Did he hurt you while I was gone? Did you wonder what it would be like to be with him and not me?"

Anger flashes across her face. "What the hell are you talking about? Of course not! I love you, Tim. I was angry you were always out, and I made a friend, but that doesn't mean I want him!"

I stare at her. Of course that's what she would say, but I'm not sure I can believe her. I love my wife, but there's something going on here, I can feel it. Even if she doesn't want Paul like that, I have a very good feeling he wants her.

"He loves you," I tell her, watching her face. I wish there were more light out here so I could see what she's thinking better, but even though it's dark, I can still tell her face has darkened even more.

"He cares about me as a friend," she corrects angrily. "Which was all I wanted this week when you were off ... playing with *your* new friend every single night! You didn't have the time for me, and Paul did. He actually made me feel like I mattered."

Cold rage washes over me when I hear her words. No man wants to hear his wife say another man made her feel good and special while he was out of town. I'm exhausted after a week of not enough sleep and after my speeding ticket. This has to end.

"Go in the house, Amy," I tell her. "I won't hurt him, but I need to talk to him."

She eyeballs me like she doesn't trust me, and I wouldn't either. In her eyes, I just did a 180 for no reason, and there's no way she's going to believe I'm being serious.

"Give me the clippers." She holds out her hand. "You want me to look the other way while you go talk to Paul? Give me your weapon, Tim."

I hesitate. I don't want to approach Paul without something to scare him off with, but it's not like he's a young man. Chances are incredibly good that I would come out on top if something were to happen between us. Even though I don't really want to, I give Amy the clippers.

"Good." She clutches them to her chest. "Do you think I should call the police?"

That's the last thing I think she should do. "No, I'm sorry I overreacted," I tell her. It's a lie. I'm not sorry, and I'm not overreacting. I know the signs of an affair, and I honestly believe Paul has been moving in for my wife. My blood boils, and it's taking all my self-control not to scream at her now, but she's not the one I'm really angry with, and I have to remember that. I'm angry with Paul, and soon I'll find him and show him just how pissed off I am.

"You'll be safe?"

I nod. "Just go in the house and lock the door, okay? I'll come bang on the front door when Paul and I have talked. I'm just going to ask him to leave, Amy, that's all."

She opens her mouth to argue, but I pin her in place with a stare.

"Fine," she shoots back at me. "You want to take my one friend from me? Fine. You're a selfish asshole, Tim, you know that?"

Turning, she hurries up the stairs to the front porch. I hear her sob, but I don't move until she's entered the house. I don't hear her throw the lock, but I'm in too much of a hurry to wait for it. She'll do what I told her to, I'm sure of it. Amy can be angry with me all she wants, but it's my job to protect her and the house. I can't do that if Paul is running around here behind my back, spending so much alone time with my wife.

I'll do what I told Amy. I'm going to ask him to leave, tell him he's not wanted. I'll give him until tomorrow to move out, I'm not a monster, and then when Amy and I go to bed tonight, everything will be okay.

Turning, I look down the garden at the cottage. He's probably in there right now, probably waiting to see what I'm going to do. I have to stand up for my house and my wife. There's no way I can let him continue to disrespect me by spending so much time alone with Amy.

But I don't want to go down there without a weapon. I told Amy I wouldn't hurt Paul, but if push comes to shove, then I'm going to be the one walking away from all this.

There are a few more garden tools in the shed I might be able to use if we get into a fight, and I hurry around the side of the house to see what else is there. From here I can see straight into the cottage window, and I pause.

He's not in there.

The back of my neck prickles, and I feel the hair stand on end. I suddenly feel exposed standing out here without a weapon, but when I reach the toolshed, I find that it's locked. "It didn't have a lock on it a few minutes ago," I say, then whip around, pressing my back up against it when I realize what that means.

Paul was here. He locked it so I couldn't get a weapon to protect myself.

"He's evil," I whisper, convincing myself I need to do something. "You can't let him hurt Amy."

I spin away from the toolshed, but not towards the front of the house. I need to handle this outside, where I can make sure he won't get his hands on my wife. I'm sure he's very good about putting his tools away when he's done, but everyone makes mistakes.

He might have left something outside.

I think about Amy wanting to call the cops, and I shake my head. There's no way I want them here telling me I'm overreacting. I need to settle this with Paul, but I have a very good feeling he's not going to want to sit and talk like adults.

I need to protect myself.

And my wife.

It's only when I turn the corner around the house that I see something I've never seen before.

I don't come around this way, not only because I have better things to do than work my way around the exterior of our home through a garden that needs a lot of TLC, but also because I didn't think there was a reason to.

That's why I've never realized there was a door to the basement from the garden.

But I see it now.

It's open with the wind, swinging back and forth slightly in the stiff breeze, and even though there's a voice screaming at me, I don't need to get distracted about what I'm doing right now. I walk towards the door and step inside.

32

PAUL

I can't find Tim.

I watched him argue with Amy, watched him spin away from the front of the house like he had a fire lit under his ass and needed to do something drastic. I tracked him around the side of the house, but then I got distracted, looking through the windows of the house for Amy, and that was when I lost sight of him.

I should have followed him. I know that now. I know I never should have let him out of my sight, not when he was so upset, not when he was running around the side of the house, probably looking for another weapon he could use against me.

But I closed and locked the toolshed when I took out a larger pair of clippers to replace the little snips I had in my pocket before, and then hid.

That was when I saw Amy standing in the window, looking out. She had one hand pressed up against the glass, and even though I was hiding in the bushes far enough away she couldn't see me, I saw the pain etched on her face.

Tim gave her that pain. Her husband is the reason she's

locked in her house right now, looking sadder than ever. He's the reason she turned to me, time and time again, when she needed someone to take care of her. He's the reason Wilma is dead, and he's going to slowly kill Amy, too, if I don't stop him.

But then where the hell did he go?

I move quickly, hurrying around the side of the house, fully expecting to see Tim doing his best to get into the tool-shed. In my mind I can just picture him slamming his fists into it over and over to break into it, but he won't be able to.

But what I see is worse.

"No," I whisper. The door is open. The door, the one through which anyone can get under the house, swings free in the wind like a kite. I don't know if it was open and Tim was just lucky enough to stumble across it, or if Tim went looking for it and found it somehow.

I doubt the latter. He might not even be in there.

But I have to know.

I inch along the side of the house, pressing myself up against the wall as I turn around the corner and peer in the door. From here I can't see anything, and I know I'm going to have to go in there to look for Tim. I can't just leave him in there to find ...

Everything.

The clippers feel good in my hand. They're a nice weight, and I heft them as I hurry through the door, pulling it shut behind me. It's dark down here, but when my eyes adjust, I see a faint glow ahead of me.

Tim must have a flashlight. I'm surprised he hasn't called the police, but from what he told Amy, he wants to handle me on my own. As quietly as possible, I hurry towards the soft glow, keeping bent over a little in case he hears me and swings the light in my direction.

Reaching the ladder I use to climb up into the house, I

reach up and lightly touch the first rung. It's easy to stretch up and flip the trapdoor open so I can climb, and I do that, prepared to go into the house. I could go to Amy. It would be easy to leave Tim down here and go to her to make sure she's okay. I'm half-tempted to do just that, but then I hear Tim swear.

"What the hell is all this?" he rages, the words like bombs from his lips.

I let go of the ladder, gripping my clippers tighter as I hurry towards him.

He hears me, or senses me. At the last minute, right when I'm about to burst into the little room where I have my shrine to Wilma and Amy set up, he wheels around, shining the flashlight right into my eyes.

I gasp, throwing up my hands, then fumble against the wall for the light switch. As soon as I flick it on, it bathes the small room in a bright light.

Tim steps back from me, holding a small keychain flashlight out in front of him like a weapon. "You're a psycho," he tells me, breathing hard. "All her things! I thought she was just misplacing them, but you were taking them all along! What the hell were you going to do to her, you freak?"

Tim has Amy's perfume bottle in his hand, and he weighs it slightly before suddenly throwing it at me. I duck, and it shatters on the wall behind me, the thick scent immediately filling the small space.

"I'm protecting her!" I scream, slowly stepping around the room, hoping he'll come out from behind the table. He's using it as a shield to protect himself, and I don't like it.

"Protecting her from what?" He moves with me, keeping the table between us.

I notice he's still gripping the flashlight in his hand, and it doesn't look like he found another weapon on his way here, and I doubt he's had time to call the police. I have the advantage. I can end this.

"From you," I snarl, pausing to stare at him. "You're going to end up killing her, Tim, just like you killed my wife!"

He blinks in surprise, then frowns again. "What the hell are you talking about? Have you lost your mind? I don't know your wife!"

"Wilma Dorner," I say, moving again to keep him from getting too comfortable. I know there's no way he's going to let me get close to him, and I don't want him to feel like he has an advantage by posting up behind the table. "When you were first hired at TechCorp, Marie gave you folders and told you to fire someone."

He goes pale. "How the hell do you know that?"

"Amy told me everything. She told me how you were too afraid to even look at the folders. You were too chickenshit to even consider whose life you were going to ruin, weren't you? You just chose one randomly, just like you would casually pick something from a menu."

He shakes his head. "I have no idea who your wife was, Paul, but I think I would know if I killed someone. What the hell does my job have to do with her?"

I step closer. My hand cramps from gripping the clippers so tightly, but I don't want to release them for a break. I want to be ready for anything Tim might do.

"You fired me," I tell him, and shock registers on his face. "You fired me, not caring that I was a good employee, that I worked my ass off, or that I was the one with health insurance."

He shakes his head and opens his mouth to argue, but I'm not interested in hearing the little excuses he comes up with.

"Wilma had cancer," I tell him, still moving slowly towards him.

He's stopped moving like he's stuck in place and is just

staring at me now, his mouth dropped slightly open in surprise.

"And when I lost my insurance, she lost her treatment. We lost everything, Tim, including our house." I pause. "This house."

"What?" The word is a whisper, like he's too shocked to put any effort behind speaking it. There's a crease between his eyebrows as he stares at me, confused, but if he would just pay attention, he would understand everything.

But that's the problem with Tim. He doesn't want to pay attention, and he certainly doesn't want to know what he did to my wife. To me. To my family.

"I wanted to hurt Amy so I could punish you," I tell him, taking another step closer. "But then I realized she's innocent in all this, Tim. You're the one who needs to be punished. You're the one who needs to die."

His face pales. He heard my words, I'm sure of it, but I'm not convinced he understands.

I'm close enough to see the small beads of sweat on his forehead, and it's now I finally lunge at him.

33

AMY

Something's terribly wrong. I know it. I pace through the house, walking from the kitchen to the living room and then back, passing the staircase in the foyer before making the circuit again.

Tim wouldn't have given up his weapon that easily, I'm sure of it. And Paul ran when Tim got home just like I told him to.

It's like they both know something I don't.

I'm about to keep walking through the house when I think I hear something. It's faint, more like a forgotten whisper than anything else, but something about it makes me shiver.

I turn, looking at the door under the stairs. Tim and I both noticed it when we first moved in, but we couldn't figure out a way to open it. Something about the door has always bothered me, though, and I walk over to it, running my hands along the edge of the door and pressing against it to see if it'll pop open.

Nothing.

"But where do you lead?" I ask. I spread my hands flat on

the door. It feels cool, like there's fresh air back there, even though the rest of the house is warm. I'm about to walk away from the little door when I think I hear a scream.

It sounds like it came from within the walls.

"What the hell?" I ask, leaning down and pressing my ear against the door. Surely I'm wrong, surely there wasn't a sound, but I'd have sworn I heard something.

I'm probably just paranoid knowing Tim and Paul are going to ... going to what? Tim was pissed, definitely more upset than I thought he had a right to be, but I have no idea how Paul will react when my husband goes to talk to him. He seems laid-back and was definitely supportive when I needed him, but if Tim goes at him angry, wanting to fight, then I don't know what's going to happen.

I turn away from the door, my heart pounding hard, but before I can decide what to do or where to go, I hear another scream.

Tim.

He's not one to scream unless he's in a lot of pain, and I turn back, pressing my ear up against the door. I have no idea where this thing goes, but I do know I need to get through it and find out. "Tim!" I scream, pounding my fist on the door. "Tim, where are you?"

No answer.

I have to get through this door. I know it sounds insane, but my husband is through there somewhere, and he's screaming. If I don't get to him, then something terrible might happen to him.

"I'm coming!" I scream again, banging on the door. When I spin away from it, my head pounds, but I know I need to hurry. I run to the kitchen to look for something—anything—that I can use to get through that door. My eyes fall on the knife block by the stove, and I grab the biggest knife we have, running back to the door with it held at my side.

I fit the tip of the blade into the crack around the door and throw my weight against it, but the tip just snaps off, and I drop the knife.

"Fuck!" Spinning around, I race to the kitchen and start opening drawers frantically, hoping to find something else I can use. I know Tim wanted me to keep the drawers clear of junk, and all I'm finding are things like scotch tape and rubber bands.

Until I remember the toolbox under the kitchen sink.

Dropping to my knees, I throw open the lid and paw through it until I find a claw hammer and a flathead screwdriver. I stare at them in my hands before heading back to the door. Dropping the hammer, I fight the tip of the screwdriver into the crack where I had the knife, then pull back, leaning hard on it as I yank on the door.

At first, nothing happens.

Then I feel the door give way a little. There's the groaning of old metal as the hinges start to tear away from the wall, and I pull harder, putting all my weight into it.

The door cracks, splinters of wood flying off as I work the screwdriver deeper. "Come on, come on," I mutter, yanking hard one more time.

That's all it takes.

I gasp as I fall back, the door popping open enough for me to grab the edge and pull it free. The hinges are so old they practically crumble under my fingers and fall to the ground at my feet. I finally free enough that I can look through the doorway.

Cool air blows into my face, and I fumble my phone from my pocket, turning on the flashlight and holding my arm through the door so I can see.

What's back there makes my blood run cold.

Double walls. The house has double walls, and we never knew it. All the times I thought someone was watching me? It's possible they were standing in between the walls.

My gaze drifts down, and I feel my breath catch in my throat.

An opening in the floor leads straight down. Pieces of wood are nailed into the wall to form a ladder.

Someone could have used the ladder to enter the house, to get into the walls. This little door would let them into the foyer if they wanted to come in that way. I stumble back.

"Oh, my God," I say, picking up the knife with my free hand. I have no idea if I'm going to need it or even if I can use it, but there's no way I can leave it here, not with the screaming I heard.

I have to find my husband. Even after all we've been through, after all I think he's done this week, he's still my husband. And what about Paul? I can't fathom the thought of Tim hurting him, but that might be what's about to happen.

Angling my body and turning around, I hold the knife between my teeth and then slowly descend the ladder. I'm trying not to think about the fact that someone could get behind the walls of my house. I'm trying not to think about the hole in the kitchen wall, the missing items Tim says I've misplaced.

Someone has been watching me, and I knew it.

As quickly and carefully as possible, I work my way down the ladder. I'm gripping my phone in one hand and carefully finding each rung before putting my full weight on it.

I can't fall.

I have to save Tim. I have to save Tim. I have to save Tim.

Those five words keep running through my head as I descend, moving faster now that I feel like I'm getting my footing under me. I could still slip, but I'm praying I won't. My teeth clamp down hard around the knife so I don't drop it, and I taste the metallic tang of it on my tongue.

Within moments, I'm out of the wall and dropping down through the floor. When my feet hit solid ground, I stop, grabbing the ladder for support and breathing hard. A light coming from my left makes me turn off my flashlight and pocket my phone. I crouch, moving slowly towards the glow, the knife held out in front of me.

Like I really know what to do with it.

Like I could really stab someone.

"What did you think was going to happen?" Paul's voice rips through the air.

I stop suddenly, the taste of bile in the back of my throat.

"Did you think you could kill my wife and get away with it? Did you really think I would leave Amy unprotected so you could hurt her, too?"

What the hell is he talking about?

I know I need to keep moving, need to get to Tim and see what I can do to help, but I honestly feel stuck in place. I can't move, can't seem to lift one foot and put it in front of the other. Paul is silent.

Is Tim still alive? What did Paul mean when he said my husband killed his wife?

It can't be true. I don't know what really happened, but I do know none of this can be true. Tim wouldn't hurt anyone, and if he did, I don't think he'd be able to keep it from me.

Right?

Before I have a chance to think about what's going on, Tim's voice fills the air, and what he says gives me chills.

34

TIM

"I didn't know she would die," I manage to gasp out. I'm flat on my back, doing my best not to scream out in pain again. I don't know what else to say to Paul to make him stop hurting me. He stands over me, a dark look on his face, the clippers in his hand. They drip blood.

My blood.

I have one hand clamped down hard over my side to stem the bleeding, but just touching my body causes pain to shoot through me. I need to press down harder to stop the bleeding. I need professional help.

But I'm certain Paul won't let me move. He's crazy. I was right about something going on this week. I was right to worry about him getting too close to Amy. Right now he's staring at me like he's never hated anyone more.

"You didn't know she would die because you didn't take the time to check out who you were firing," Paul tells me, bending down so he can get a better look at me. He presses the tip of the clippers up under my chin, forcing me to look at him. I do, the cool metal against my soft skin enough to make me want to throw up.

"It was too much to ask me to do it," I tell him, swallowing hard. "Marie told me—"

"Marie didn't have the balls to do it! If you had just looked in my file, Tim, you would have known the truth! You would have known firing me would kill Wilma, but you didn't care enough to look, did you? You didn't care, you didn't look, and now my sweet wife is dead."

Fear washes over me. I never met Paul before I fired him, never even paid attention to the names on the folders until I hastily chose one and handed it to Marie. All I knew was it was too much to ask of me, and I panicked.

I chose a file, and apparently I chose wrong.

"Please don't hurt me," I whisper, pushing harder on my wound. "I'm sorry, Paul. I'll do whatever you want, but please don't hurt me. Let me go; let Amy go. We'll leave you alone, okay?"

"That's not enough." He crouches, then sits on my stomach. Any other time I'd have been able to buck my hips up and throw him off, but there's no way I can do that now, not with the pain I'm in.

"I have to save Amy. I have to protect her from you." His voice is quiet, and he leans forward, so I can smell his breath washing over me. "You don't get that yet, do you? I have to save Amy, have to keep her from suffering at your hands."

I shake my head, wanting nothing more than to get my point across. "I wouldn't ever hurt her. You have to see that! She's everything to me, and I love her."

"I loved Wilma." His answer comes fast like he was fully expecting what I was going to say. "I loved my wife, but that didn't stop you from killing her, did it? You ruined my life, Tim. I was going to kill Amy and ruin yours, but then I changed my mind."

"What?" I can't believe what he just said, even though he said this once before. "What did you just say?"

"I was going to kill your wife, just like you killed mine." He grins at me like we're sharing some joke together. "I thought it would be a great way to make you feel what I felt when I lost the woman I promised to love for the rest of my life. I thought it would be good for you to see how terrible life can be when someone takes what you love."

My heart pounds like a trapped bird. Even though my side still hurts, all I can do is focus on Paul's face. I should have recognized his name. I should have paid more attention to whose folder I gave Marie so many years ago. I should have done whatever I could to protect Amy, but now this psychopath has us, and I don't know if he's going to let her survive after he kills me.

Because I'm sure that's what he's going to do.

"Don't you dare hurt Amy."

"No, Tim, I won't, and you want to know why? Because you do a good enough job of hurting her yourself! What do you think her week was like while you were off in Raleigh, out drinking every night? She was devastated. You ruin all good things, Tim, and it's time for you to stop. I love her. I'm going to take care of her forever."

He pushes the clippers harder against my neck. I have no doubt he's going to kill me here, and I let go of my side, reaching up for his face. My fingers sink into the skin on his cheeks as I try to push him off me.

"You don't deserve her!" he screams, twisting his head out of the way so my hands fall from his face.

It hurts to move, hurts more to try to push him off me, but I can't just lie here on the ground, waiting for him to kill me.

"You never did! She's too good for you!"

"Amy!" I think my wife is still in the house. She hasn't come looking for me, but I scream for her anyway, hoping she can hear me. "Amy! Call the police!"

"You think she'd choose you over me?" Paul raises his hand over his head.

I wince at the sight of the clippers. All he has to do is bring them down. All he has to do is slam them into my chest and I'll be dead, and Amy will never know what really happened to me.

I love her, but this week she got closer to Paul. I wouldn't ever hurt her again, but she didn't wait before running right into his arms. I was so careful this week, always making sure I honored my vows to her, but can she say she did the same?

It feels like time slows down. I see the way Paul's face twists with anger and excitement, but then he stops, his eyes flicking up from me. As much as I want to turn to see what he's looking at, I can't, not with him pressing me down into the floor.

It's hard for me to even take a deep breath, let alone contort my body so I can look behind me.

"No. What are you doing here?" Paul breathes the words into the air.

I feel my heart start to beat faster. I have no way of knowing if it's Amy behind me, but if she's here, then she needs to leave.

How can I trust that Paul isn't going to hurt her too?

"Amy," I say, but my voice is too quiet, and I'm sure she can't hear me calling her.

"This was never the plan!" Amy screams.

I crane my head to the side, trying to get a glimpse of what's going on. At the same time, Paul shifts off me. I gasp in a breath, the wound in my side making tears stream down my face, but I try to ignore it.

Before either of them remembers that I'm here, I roll over, pushing myself up onto my knees and my palms. Each movement is excruciating, sending more blood running down my side. I want to scream from the pain, but I know I have to get out of here.

If I heard my wife correctly, then she was in on this little plan of his. If I heard her correctly, then I need to run to save myself.

35

PAUL

"I'll kill you if you touch him again. I thought you were here to protect me, to keep me safe. I thought you were my friend." Amy's voice is low and dangerous, the sound of it cutting through the silence that's growing between us.

Shock rolls through me as I stare at her.

"You'll kill me?" I laugh, tightening my grip on the clippers. I've stepped away from Tim, no longer caring what happens to him. I'll deal with him once I make Amy understand that I love her. "You'll kill me for protecting you? For keeping you company when your husband was too busy? For watching you to make sure you were always safe?"

"You were supposed to just be our caretaker. You were supposed to be our friend." Her voice drops to a whisper. "You were watching me?" She keeps her eyes on me as she inches closer to Tim, only looking away from me for a moment as she drops down to her knees next to him.

I don't look at her face. My eyes are locked on the knife she's holding. I have no idea how she found us, how she managed to get in here to stop what I'm about to do, but I don't want to be angry at her.

I'm mad at her husband. He's the reason everything is happening as it is. If he hadn't killed Wilma, I never would have lost the house.

This is all Tim's fault.

She looks up from her husband, catching me staring at her. "You were watching me from behind the walls!" She points the knife at me.

The tip of it has broken off, and I finally tear my eyes from her weapon to look at her face.

"You were! All this time I thought you were my friend, you were spying on me!"

"I was protecting you!" I scream, hoping she'll understand. I don't want to yell at Amy. I don't want to scare her or hurt her. "I was there when Tim was too busy for you, or did you forget? I was there when he was out partying and you were left at home alone. He left you in this house where anything could have happened, but I wasn't going to let you get hurt!"

"You're the only one who would have hurt me!" Amy screams back. She's on her feet, her eyes dark with rage.

Fear mingles with anger in her voice, and my jaw drops when I look at her. Her eyes are narrow slits, her grip on the knife so tight the handle could snap. She's taut like a bow, quivering with rage, and I'm not sure what she'll do next.

"I never would have hurt you." Stepping closer to her, I move slowly, one hand out in front of me in case she lunges towards me with the knife. I keep my voice calm now so I don't spook her. I want to show Amy how much she means to me. "All the times I watched you, all the times I kept an eye on you ... it was just to make sure you were safe."

"You were spying on me!" Amy hisses. She brandishes her

knife to stop me approaching. "Did you watch me change? Were you watching me in the shower?"

"No!" The word bursts from me, and I hope she can tell how truthful I'm being. "No, I didn't do that. I wouldn't have done that. All I wanted to do was make sure you were safe. I was protecting you, which was more than Tim was doing. He was off partying, and you needed someone there with you."

"I didn't."

"You did," I tell her. For the first time since I changed my plan, from wanting to hurt her to get to Tim to wanting to protect her and kill her husband, I falter, unsure of what I'm doing. I have to make her realize how much I care for her. I have to get it through her head that I love her, that she has to be mine. She's not replacing Wilma, but she's filling that void in my life. "You told me you wished you weren't alone."

"You're insane," she whispers and shakes her head like she's trying to clear it. "I never wanted you to come into our house. I never asked you to watch me." Understanding dawns on her face. I see it clear as day as her expression changes from rage to horror. "You were watching me through the kitchen wall, weren't you? You're the one who took my jewelry. My perfume. The photo."

I don't want to answer that only because she doesn't understand why I did what I did. She doesn't seem to see that everything I did, all the sleep I lost to watch her, all the times I stood silently in the wall to keep an eye on her—it was all for her.

For the first time since finding me with Tim, she glances around the room, her expression changing when she sees the altar I have set up for her. "What is this?" she whispers, walking over to finger her necklace.

I hold my breath as she takes it all in. Her eyes widen at the careful way I've set it all up, at how everything is positioned perfectly. Surely she sees the beauty in it, the love.

"I did it for you." She has to see that. I need her to know I changed my plans for her. I stayed awake nights for her. I stood until my legs wanted to give out just for her. "It wasn't the plan, you know. I changed it for you."

"You changed the plan?" She sounds incredulous. "Watching me through the walls of the house wasn't your original plan? Was your first one not creepy enough?"

I eyeball her, trying to decide what I'm going to say. I thought she could handle this. I honestly thought she'd understand what I'd done, that she'd see I was protecting her from Tim, but now I'm not so sure. Maybe it was all too fast. Maybe she didn't have enough time to realize how much she means to me and how happy she could be with me.

My palms are suddenly sweaty, and I wipe them on my pants.

Did I make a mistake in changing the plan? Should I have gone ahead with the original one? That's what Holly wants, but I don't. I'm willing to upset my daughter to have Amy.

"What are you going to do now?" Her voice breaks through my concentration. "You're going to kill Tim and then what? Do you think you and I are going to live happily ever after with you staring at me through the walls in my house all the time?"

"It's my house!" I don't mean to yell at her, but the words burst out of me before I can stop them. "My house! I lived here with Wilma until your husband killed her!" I turn to point at Tim, but when I do, a chill races through my body, and I stumble forward, reaching for the wall for support.

He's not there.

36

AMY

I *have to protect my husband.*

That thought keeps running through my head, and I know I'll do anything to keep him safe. Seeing him stretched out on the ground like that, blood staining his shirt ... I shake my head, doing my best to clear it because I know I need to keep my head in the game right now if I want to protect him.

I might be angry at him, but that doesn't mean I don't love him.

"Where did he go?" Paul's voice is tight and full of terror, and my eyes flick to the ground where my husband was just a moment ago. He's not there, but there's blood trailing the ground, and I feel my stomach twist.

"Where did he go?" Paul screams before turning to look at me. His eyes are wide enough to see the white around his irises. He's breathing heavily and has bright spots of color in his cheeks. When I don't answer, he steps towards me. I hold my knife up in response.

"Stay back," I tell him, aiming it at him. Could I cut him? I have no idea.

All I know is Tim is gone, and I need to get out, too. Though I don't know if I'll leave here in one piece.

"Amy," Paul says, rolling my name around in his mouth like that's going to calm me down, "you've got to see this is all a mistake, right? You've got to see I did this all for you."

"Did what?" I scream the question at him. "Stabbed my husband? Watched me while I was ..." I almost can't finish the sentence, it's too terrible, but I force the words out of my mouth. "Watched me while I was sleeping? What the hell's wrong with you?"

"I was protecting you. I love you." He still has the clippers in his hand, but I can see he's relaxed his grip. I know that doesn't mean he won't hurt me, but the fear eating at me lessens. "It's not like your husband was willing to protect you, was he? Where is he now, anyway?"

He's playing on my fears, and I know that, but I still glance around the space nervously. Tim isn't here. He was. He'd been stabbed and was hurt, and I came to his aid, but he left when I saw the altar.

"He left you here, just like he's always going to leave you." Paul takes a step towards me. "Put down the knife, Amy, and let's talk about this. You have to see it from my side. You're not stupid; you had to have known this was coming."

"That what was coming?"

"That Tim would turn tail and run the moment you really needed him. That someday something would happen and he'd be unable to protect you. That he wouldn't even be willing to try. You need someone to protect you, Amy. I can do that. I'm the only one here who is willing to do that, don't you see it?"

"No." I whisper the word, and when he takes another step towards me, I automatically step back. The thought of being close to him is enough to make my stomach turn. There's blood on his clippers—my husband's blood—and I'm having trouble tearing my eyes away from it.

"You see it." Paul isn't slowing down. He keeps moving closer to me, forcing me to take more steps away from him.

It smells like me in this room, and when I step on something that crunches, I glance down to see my perfume bottle shattered on the floor. I feel like I'm going to be sick. My head feels like it's floating, and I shake it a little to try to clear it.

"I'll do anything to keep you safe," Paul tells me.

Thank God he's stopped coming towards me now. I don't think I could handle him being any closer than he is, but he's still staring at me like he's waiting for an answer.

"Tim doesn't deserve you, Amy. You need someone who loves you to take care of you."

"And that's you?" I find my voice again. "You think you're the right person to keep me safe when you couldn't even protect your wife?"

"What?" His voice is a hiss, and he reminds me of a snake getting ready to strike.

I reach behind me, my fingers brushing against the wall, and silently curse that I'm not closer to the door. I can't very well turn around right now and look for the door. I can't take my eyes off him. I don't trust him.

"If you loved Wilma, you would have saved her life." It's a terrible thing to say to him and I know it, but I need him to back off. Somehow, I have to get him to leave me alone, to stop whatever madness has taken over in his mind. "You would have done anything you could have to make sure she was safe and healthy, but you didn't, did you?"

His jaw tightens, as does his grip on the clippers. "I gave up everything! I lost the house. I lost our cars. I've been living off and on with my daughter while she looked for the right way to get to you! Every time someone from the bank came here, I had to go to her house and move in so nobody would know I was here. I had to stay with her while you two decided whether or not to hire a caretaker. You think I didn't do everything I could to save her? All I've done has been for you." He pauses, taking deep breaths like he's trying to calm himself.

"For me?"

He blinks. "For her. For Wilma."

I don't know what I'm trying to do here, only that I need to get out of this room. Paul terrifies me. Part of me wants to make him so angry he can't see straight, and the other part of me is afraid of what he will do if he does get to that point.

Maybe I'll be able to run if I make him that mad. He might not be able to concentrate on me, and I might be able to escape.

Or he'll kill me the way he tried to kill Tim.

"I think you tried to save her, but you failed." I'm terrified but doing my best to keep my voice as calm and even as possible. If he knows how scared I am, then he's going to use that against me, I'm sure of it. He won't stand there and wait to hear what I have to say—he'll run at me and kill me. "I think you didn't deserve to save her."

None of what I'm saying is necessarily true, but I want to make him mad enough to run at me, and that's exactly what he does. He roars, sounding more feral than ever before, and rushes me, his clippers held up above his head.

Bile tickles the back of my throat, and I lunge forward, my arm extended, closing my eyes as I pray that my knife hits him.

It does, and he screams, and I duck out of the way before he can hurt me back. Then I start running.

Adrenaline pumps through my body as I tear out from the basement. I slam into the swinging wooden door that leads outside and push it out of the way before bursting out into the cool night air. It's the first time I feel like I can breathe without sucking my perfume deep into my lungs, and I stop, grab my thighs, and take deep gasping breaths.

"You're okay," I tell myself. "You're okay, but you have to keep moving." I don't hear Paul behind me, but if he comes for me, then I need to be away from here. I need to find Tim. It's risky, but I cup my hands around my mouth and call to him. "Tim! Where are you?"

No answer. Turning uncertainly, I make up my mind and start for the house. I have to get out of here, have to get help. Maybe going to the house is a dumb idea, but I'm at a loss for what I should do. I have no idea how to save myself or where to go. Stopping short, I remember I have my cell phone tucked in my pocket. My fingers tremble as I pull it out and tap the screen to wake it up.

"Come on, come on," I mutter. My skin prickles as the wind blows, and I'm well aware I'm standing out in the middle of the garden, completely on display for anyone who might want to find me.

Paul could find me.

Swearing, I drop down to the ground and cover up my phone's screen to block the glow. I only have my phone app open and haven't called the police yet, but I don't want to draw any attention to myself right now by talking on the phone. I need to get farther away from the house, need to get somewhere where I can hide.

Not in the house, not when Paul can easily get into it and move through the double walls without anyone knowing where he is. The thought makes me shiver, and I reach down, placing my hand on the cold ground as I think.

Not the cottage, not when he might want to go down there to hide and lick his wounds.

I'm about to stand up and make a run for the woods that surround the garden just so I have someplace I can hide when I see someone slink along the side of the house. They move quickly, like they know where they're going, and my jaw drops when they slip into the door to the basement.

It wasn't Tim, that much is for sure. The person was much too petite to be my husband.

So who the hell is sneaking around my house right now? I fumble with my phone, keeping my eyes on the door to the basement. My phone slips from my hand. I lunge for it, swearing, but find it with my foot.

The cracking sound of the screen makes me wince, and I drop to my knees.

"No, no, no, this can't be happening," I say, scooping my phone up and holding it in the palm of my hand. "Come on, you're fine." I tap the screen before pushing the power button half a dozen times in an attempt to wake up my phone.

Nothing.

37

TIM

Each breath hurts. When I breathe, it feels like I'm sucking in flames, like they're licking me from the inside, burning my skin and cooking me. I have my hand pressed down hard over where Paul stabbed me, and I stumble away from the house, not knowing where I'm going, only knowing I have to put as much space between me and the house as possible.

I have to get away from Paul. I only caught a glimpse of Amy standing there when I escaped, but I didn't need to see more. She showed up to help him, I know it. They got close this week, just like I was afraid they would.

I was behaving in Raleigh, making sure I didn't cheat on her, and what did she do?

Make someone fall in love with her.

I'm not really paying attention to the ground, and one wrong step into a hole sends me sprawling forward. Throwing my hands out from my body to brace myself for the hit, I grit my teeth at the same time. I slam into the ground, my wrists aching at the impact. Pain shoots up my arms, and I roll over onto my back, but I don't get up.

At least here there's no way he can find me. I can't seem to quiet the voices in my head that are screaming at me, that I should have seen all this coming. It's not like I could have really known Paul would go insane and stab me, but he did.

My mind reels when I think about what he said.

He's the man I fired.

"No," I mumble, slowly pushing myself back onto my knees so I can stand up. "That can't be true." But if it isn't, how would he know all the details and then use them against me? And why would Amy tell him everything? I know why. She wanted to hurt me, wanted to make me feel bad about my time in Raleigh. There's something there, some nugget of truth, but I'm too terrified of him coming for me to try to wrap my mind around what it might be.

Regret washes over me like a wave when I think about how I trusted my wife this week. I knew she shouldn't be spending so much time with Paul, but how could I stop her?

I'd go back for her now, but I don't get the feeling she wants to escape. She didn't run to help me; she didn't follow me out; she didn't hurt Paul.

She didn't choose me.

Pressing my hand back over my wound, I try to ignore the way the blood oozes out between my fingers. I'm light-headed, but I don't know if that's because of how much blood I've lost or if it's because I can't seem to understand exactly how this night has gone.

"I need to get Amy," I finally say to myself, pushing up to a stand. It's stupid, but I want to know the truth. My legs are weak and wobbly like a baby deer, and I lurch forward, stumbling over rocks and sticks I thought Paul would have cleaned up by now. He should have taken care of all this mess in the garden, but then he wouldn't be able to use our property against us.

I groan, taking another step.

Amy was right all along. She knew someone was watching her from the walls, that something wasn't right with the house, but I thought she was just imagining things. I shouldn't have run right now. I should have stayed and tried to protect her, but at that moment I just knew I needed to save myself.

The door on the side of the house suddenly swings open, and I throw myself back down to the ground, a moan escaping my lips. Two figures emerge, one smaller than the other, their arms wrapped around the bigger one. Paul is limping, gripping his side in much the same way I keep holding mine.

Amy's helping him.

That thought eats at the back of my mind, and I feel my skin grow hot. She's still there, still helping this man who scared her so much. She could have run when I did, but she didn't. Rage washes over me as I watch her help him down the path to the cottage.

Why would she still be helping him?

He said he loves her. It doesn't make any sense, but I see it there in front of me, clear as day, that my wife chose him over me. It doesn't matter that it's dark out or that the clouds have mostly covered the moon, blocking out its already dim light. I see the two figures as they work their way down the path to the cottage, and rage overtakes me.

Amy made her choice.

There's a voice in the back of my head asking me what I'm going to do about it, but I shake my head to try to clear it. I honestly don't know what to do. She's with him now, taking care of whatever injury he has. I don't know what happened to him, and I don't care. All that matters is that I know she chose him over me.

"Just like she's done all week," I say. My voice surprises me, but then I speak again, still quietly, still afraid Paul might hear me and come back to try to finish the job. "She chose you all week, and she's still doing it."

I don't get it. We're married, and happy, or I thought we were. If I'm honest with myself, maybe I was happier this week in Raleigh than I've been with my wife for a while, but that doesn't mean I'm going to choose Susie over her. It doesn't mean I would put my arms around the other woman when my wife was as upset as I am now.

"You made your choice," I tell her, even though there's no way she can hear me right now. I know it's stupid, the desire to follow the two of them down to the cottage. I know I should just turn back for the house, lock myself in, and call the police, but the house isn't safe, not with Paul around.

He could get to it before I knew what he was doing. He's dangerous, that man, and even more so now that Amy is helping him. The fact that she would choose him over me so quickly, without any question, is almost enough to do me in, but I didn't get this far in life just sitting down and crying when something didn't go my way.

No, I got this far in life by not being afraid to take what I wanted.

Steeling myself, I ignore the pain that hits me when I think about my wife turning on me. I ignore the fact that I could call the police and have them here in no time to take care of the problem for me. I pretend like I'm not injured, although I keep my hand firmly on my side. Every step I take jostles my body and exacerbates the bleeding, but I ignore it, my hand plastered to my side like it's going to be enough to save me.

Because it will be.

I stumble away from the house, carefully kicking my feet

out in front of me as I go so I don't trip over something and fall again. It doesn't matter that I'm dripping blood behind me, because the people who want me dead are ahead of me, cozy in the cottage, unaware I'm coming for them.

It feels like it's taken forever to finally reach the cottage. The interior lights are all on, the light streaming out from the windows like light from a lighthouse. It should look comforting and safe, like the perfect place to go on a cold dark night, but my blood chills at the sight of it. This isn't the house of someone who will invite you in for a cup of tea.

It's the house of an evil warlock who lives in the woods. Paul's the warlock, and his goal has been to take Amy away from me.

The sound of low voices reaches me as I inch my way closer to the cottage. Approaching it at an angle, I grab the windowsill and carefully lean over, doing my best to look into the room without being seen.

I can't see Amy from here, but I see Paul. He's at the little table, his feet spread out in front of him like he needs extra support to keep him from falling over even though he's collapsed in a chair. One hand is gripping his side just like I'm holding mine, the other is holding a glass of a dark amber liquid.

He takes a sip and slowly removes his hand from his side, looking down at it before shaking his head. "That really hurt," he says, but Amy doesn't respond.

Where is she? I know she went in there with him. There's no way she would help him out of the basement of our house like that and then abandon him halfway to the cottage. She's just not the type of person to leave someone to fend for themselves when she's around to help them.

Unless she isn't in there helping him.

Unless she's out here looking for me.

The hair on the back of my neck stands up, and I whip around, no longer interested in looking through the cottage window to see what's going on inside. I need to find my wife before she finds me.

38

PAUL

Holly turns from her spot at the sink and holds up the wet rag in her hand. "Lucky thing I decided to come by and see you when you missed our little nightly check-in again, Dad. Let me clean that for you and get you patched up. It doesn't look like she hit any major organs, or you wouldn't have been able to walk down here." Her smile is all teeth, no mirth, and it doesn't reach her eyes.

"You're all heart," I tell her, shifting position and lifting up my shirt so she can see the wound. "I'll have to go to the hospital eventually, though."

"They'll report the stabbing," she says, walking over to me. She dabs lightly at the wound, and I hiss, the pain shooting through my body. "You'll have to answer questions."

"I'll have to answer them anyway."

This makes her look up at me, the rag in her hand hovering over the wound. It's turning bright red, and she probably needs to rinse it out and start fresh, but we don't have a lot of time to do this. I need to get back out there and figure out what's wrong with Amy. All week she's turned to me to take care of her and protect her, and I've done just that.

Now that Holly is here, the stakes have just got higher. My daughter wants Amy dead, and this little song and dance she and I are doing is already getting old.

I'm exhausted from all the long nights watching Amy sleep and making sure she didn't get hurt. I'm tired of listening to her conversations with Tim and knowing full well she deserves someone who will take better care of her.

And this is how she repays me?

"Hold this here," Holly says, pulling me from my thoughts.

Putting my fingers where she directs, I press down hard, the pain causing a bright flash of light to appear behind my eyes.

"I'm going to use gauze and then tape to keep it in place. What's the play here, Dad? What are you hoping to accomplish?"

Her hair falls around her face like a curtain when she asks those questions, and I know she's just trying to protect herself from the answers. She used to do that all the time when she was a little girl, pull her hair down between the two of us. It was her way of steeling herself against whatever answer she might get, knowing she wouldn't like it. I can't help but be surprised she's still doing it.

"I have to save her," I tell my daughter. It's the only thing that makes sense to me, and I'm surprised she's even questioning it.

Her hand hovers over my body, and her eyes snap up to meet mine. When she speaks, her voice is harsh. "You were going to kill her to punish him. You were going to show him what it was like for us when we lost Mom. You promised me."

"I know," I tell her, taking her wrist and squeezing it, "but plans change. This is better, believe me. I want to punish Tim and make sure he can't hurt other people. If we just take Amy from him, it will hurt, but it won't stop him. The only way to stop him is to kill him."

Holly shakes her head and yanks her wrist from my grasp. Her mouth has fallen open slightly, and she's looking at me like she's never seen me before. "You can't be serious."

"Plans change. Sometimes that's the only way to make something happen. We want to stop Tim. We have to actually stop him, not just give him a villain origin story."

"No, you need to make him suffer." She pauses, chewing on her lower lip for a moment. "You're only backing out because you feel something for her. You know what? How about this? We'll kill them both."

"What? No." I shake my head, not wanting to give my daughter any more ammunition than she already has. If she knows I have feelings for Amy, that looking at her makes me miss Wilma less ... I know what Holly would do, and I can't let her. "You've got it all wrong. Killing him is the best way to stop him. The only way."

"No." Taking a step back from me, she points at me, her finger against my chest like she wants to stab me there and end this argument.

There's a flash of anger in her eyes that makes rage flare up in me. Why can't she see I'm doing what's best? Why does she have to make everything more difficult than it needs to be?

"You're doing this because you have a soft spot for her."

I have to end this nonsense. Standing hurts, but sitting down in this chair and letting my daughter talk to me like this isn't a good option. Gritting my teeth, I force myself up, grabbing hard onto the edge of the table for support. I waver just a little, but Holly sees it, I'm sure she does.

"If you're not going to go through with killing them both, then I'll do it." Her voice is soft, so soft, I'll have to lean closer to hear her, but I don't move. The cottage is so still and silent

I could hear the smallest whisper she makes. "She tried to kill you, Dad. Do you really think she's going to love you after this?"

"I don't want her to love me," I lie, the pain of the words almost matching the throbbing in my side. If I don't want her to love me, then what the hell am I doing? Why am I looking out for her the way that I am? Why am I doing everything I can to protect her? Questions swirl through my head, and I know I need to slow down and focus on them to figure out the answers, but I can't, not now, not with Holly looking at me like I've lost my mind.

If I want to protect Amy and keep her safe, then I have to protect her not only from Tim, but also my daughter.

A chill runs up my spine.

It's almost too much to think about the implications of that.

Can I do what needs to be done?

"You wouldn't hurt me to save her, would you?" She backs up a little bit, dropping the tape and gauze in her hand on the kitchen counter.

The clippers I used to stab Tim are right there, just a few inches from her hand, but she doesn't reach for them.

Not yet, anyway.

"No," I tell her. "No, you're my daughter. I love you, Holly. I wouldn't do anything to hurt you." It's a lie, just another lie to go along with all the others. I would hurt Holly to save Amy, but my daughter can't know that.

"You are hurting me!" Her hand flinches towards the clippers, and I wince. "By not ending this, you are hurting me!"

"We can figure this out." Holding out my hands between the two of us, I take a step closer to her. "Holly, we can talk this out and figure out what we're going to do. Nobody has to get hurt besides Tim."

"No, we're going to kill them both." The expression on her face scares me. "Tim and Amy."

I think back to watching Amy through the walls. She's so innocent, so sweet. Holly was like that when she was younger, but then the world made her hard. She doesn't need anyone to protect her. She protects herself and isn't afraid of handling whatever comes her way.

But Wilma stayed sweet until the end. Just like I wanted to protect my wife, I need to protect Amy.

My daughter doesn't need me like that.

Problems at work? Holly takes care of it. A date gets too handsy for her liking? She handles it. She's stronger than Amy and doesn't need me to watch out for her like she did when she was a little girl. I was so busy throwing myself into my career before I was fired that I wasn't home much. When Wilma got sick, I spent all my free time taking care of her in the few years before she died. All that time, Holly was growing up, and I never really noticed how quickly that happened. Now she doesn't need me to watch out for her.

But Amy does. Holly is strong enough to handle whatever happens to her, whether she likes it or not. She doesn't need someone fighting her battles or watching over her to make sure nobody hurts her in the middle of the night. She doesn't need a man to keep an eye on her when she's gotten into a fight with someone, because Holly never loses fights.

Amy does. She needs someone to look out for her, and while that person really should be Tim, it's not. He's not willing, not able, and not strong enough to protect her. If I had someone like Amy to protect, I'd never let them get hurt.

And I *do* have someone like that to protect.

I have Amy.

And that's why I know what I have to do.

39

AMY

"Tim!" I whisper-yell my husband's name as I slowly work my way back up to the house. I'm honestly terrified to stand up and call out to him. What if Paul were to hear me? Or the mystery person who appeared at the house right when he needed them? I saw the two work their way down to the cottage, both of them moving slowly but with purpose.

I have no idea how long they're going to be down there or who Paul has with him, but right now at least I know where I can go. I can go up to the house, although I'm not sure I'll ever be comfortable entering it again. Knowing Paul was watching me from behind the walls when I was so afraid of that very thing happening ... a shiver shoots up my spine, and I rub my hands over my arms.

Which reminds me of the knife I'm still clutching in my right hand. I didn't think Paul would really run into it, but I had goaded him on, forced him to do it. Tears spring to my eyes when I think about what I said to him, and a sob escapes me before I can clamp a hand down over my mouth to stop any others from slipping past my lips.

I thought he loved me. Not like *that*, not in the way Tim was so afraid I was loving him. I don't want to have an affair with Paul, but I want him around. He reminds me of my dad, or who I wanted my dad to be when I was growing up, but Paul wasn't acting like a good dad.

He was watching me. Following me. Listening in on my conversations and making my skin crawl when I thought I was all alone. I stop walking, turning back to the cottage to make sure nobody is coming up behind me. The light from the windows looks so cheery that I want to run down there and throw the door open.

I remember how happy and comfortable I felt in there with Paul when he made dinner, how much I loved the little cottage the first time I saw it.

I also remember how terrified I'd been when I realized there had been a cup of steaming tea on the table.

Shaking my head, I turn back to the house. It doesn't matter how I try to spin it to myself, Paul is not a good guy. He took advantage of Tim and me, and while I had a lot of fun with him when Tim was away, I now need to find my husband and tell him I'm sorry.

I'm sorry I upset him so much by spending time with Paul.

I'm sorry he thought I wanted our caretaker instead of him.

Another sob, but this time I'm ready, and I have my hand over my mouth to stop it from escaping. When I angrily wipe the tears off my cheeks with the back of my hand, I smell the metallic scent of Paul's blood, and my stomach turns. Stopping where I am, I bend over, my stomach twisting in on itself as I retch.

"Amy."

My name comes to me on the wind, and I whip around, wiping my mouth on my arm. I heard someone call me, I'm sure of it, but I can't tell which direction it came from.

I also can't tell who it was.

"Tim?" I call, dropping back down to the ground. It was stupid of me to have stood up in the middle of the dead garden like a beacon for whoever wanted to find me. It was insane of me to think I could just stand there and Paul wouldn't come looking for me. "Tim?" My voice is quieter.

In the silence of the night I hear my heart hammering in my ears. Putting the knife down carefully next to my shoe so I can grab it again if I need to, I clamp my hands down over my ears and count to ten.

I'm hearing things, and I need to figure out how to press the reset button. Maybe if I stop listening to anything at all for a moment, I can stop the sounds and voices running through my mind.

"Amy!"

When I drop my hands, I hear it again. This time, instead of standing up and showing everyone exactly where I am, I grab my knife and start crawling towards the house. It feels insane, to be moving through the garden like this, but fear tickles the back of my neck, working its way down my spine, fingers of it spreading out through my body.

I'm gasping in tiny breaths of air. My ears hurt from straining to hear what's going on around me. I need to know if that was Tim calling me. Or Paul. Or if I'm just hearing things. Tim was stabbed, I don't know how bad, and there's no way for me to guess where he might be hiding.

He ran the first chance he had.

"I would have run too," I tell myself, shaking my head to clear that thought about my husband. Even as I whisper that to myself, though, I don't know if it's true. If Tim were in danger and I thought I could save him, I would have stayed.

I *did* stay. I goaded Paul into running at me so I could hurt him and make sure he couldn't hurt me or my husband any more. And what did Tim do when things got scary?

He ran. He left me there, by myself, to handle whatever Paul wanted to do to me.

I freeze, both hands on the ground, the sharp rocks pressing up into my palms and knees. I needed my husband, and he ran. He ran, just like he'd been running all week long.

Turning, I sit on the ground and pull my knees up to my chest. I wish I could call the police. I wish I hadn't broken my phone. I wish I knew if I should call out for my husband or not. He was here, and he could have protected me, but he didn't, just like he didn't try to take care of me this week, even though I needed him.

"What the hell am I going to do?" I ask the air, keeping my voice so low I can barely hear my own words. I wish I could ask someone.

Before this week, I would have turned to Tim in a heartbeat. He was always there for me, no matter if I was quitting my job to try to make it as a copywriter or if I just had a bad experience with someone at the grocery store. Never in my life did I feel like he wouldn't be there for me when I needed him.

Until this week.

And then there's Paul. He stepped up for me in a way I never imagined this week. He was there for me. *Too* there for me. He took it beyond what I wanted and what I needed, and now the thought of asking him for help terrifies me.

"Never mind the fact that you stabbed him," I mutter to myself.

And who the hell is with him in the cottage? Someone else is here, someone obviously on Paul's side. He's with someone who wants to help him, and I don't have anyone.

I could have Tim, but I don't. He left me the moment he had a chance to save himself.

I'm the only one on my side.

I'm the only one who can protect myself from these people and make sure I wake up tomorrow morning in one piece.

That's why I decide on my next move.

40

TIM

"Amy." I whisper her name into the night, hoping against hope she'll hear me and respond.

She doesn't move; nothing moves; the entire garden is still and frozen like someone cast a spell on it. It's unnerving. Gardens are supposed to be full of life and growth, and this one is dead. It's dark and broken, full of hibernating bushes that send their twisted fingers up to the sky and rocks that are cold and hard as ice littering the ground.

How we ever thought this place could be beautiful is beyond me. It's dead and decaying, a place of disease and heartache, and the only reason why Amy and I are even fighting right now.

"Amy."

Still nothing. I'm drawn to the house, to the warmth and comfort I'm sure I'll find in there, but Amy won't be there. She'll be with Paul, so that doesn't leave me many options for where she might be.

"Amy."

I don't know why I keep whispering her name into the

dark like she's suddenly going to answer me. If she is close enough to hear me, then she's not making a peep. And if she is close to me, then I should probably be more worried than I am.

I just know I need to find her, to end this, but I don't want to. She chose Paul's side. She told him everything. She helped him down to the cottage, and I have no idea what they're doing right now. Even though I know all this, it's still hard for me to see Amy as the enemy. She's so sweet, so kind, and so loving.

But someone was helping the caretaker down to his little cottage, and my wife is the only other person here. She's the only person who would wrap her arm around his waist like that and lead him to someplace he would feel safe. She's the only one who might side with a complete stranger over her husband just to prove a point.

And now I know what I have to do.

I have to get to the house and call the police. I have to get them here to stop this madness. Amy's under some sort of spell. That's the only thing that makes sense enough to explain why she would choose someone who isn't her husband over me. There's no way she would willingly side with him except for the fact that he's been lying to her.

He's been telling her things to confuse her, I'm sure of it. Paul has been doing everything he can to make Amy think he's the good guy, not me, and now she's turned on me.

So much for our wedding vows.

If she wants to play the game like this, then I'll play, too. I'll go down to the cottage and tell them everything is over. I'll let them know I just want out. They want to be together? Fine. I just want out of here. My side hurts, and I gasp as I turn down the path towards the small building.

The front door opens, and someone slips out.

Not Paul. Amy. It's obviously her, thin and short, moving

quickly and confidently like she's walked these paths all week with Paul as her guide.

She's coming for me, I know it. I watch as she hurries away from the cottage, moving like she's on a mission. Her head turns this way and that, and even though it's still too dark out to see the expression on her face, I see how she moves, like she's hunting for something.

Like she's hunting for me.

Fear rushes through me like I just took a shot of it, chilling me from the inside when I realize she's not moving like she's worried for me. Her movements are jerky and hurried, like she's on borrowed time to fix something.

Or to finish something.

I gasp and turn back towards the house, walking as fast as I can. Blood gushes out between my fingers now, my elevated heart rate pumping it faster through my body, and I press down even harder, trying to keep it from all leaking out. It's soaking my clothes and running down into my pants, the damp feeling on my skin unnerving.

I just have to get to the house. It's not safe in there, not really, and I know that now, but if I can get into the house, then I can get my phone from my jacket pocket. If I can just get to it and call the cops as quickly as possible, then it won't matter if someone else is in the house with me.

I can protect myself. I can lock myself in the kitchen with a knife for protection and stop whoever might try to hurt me. It doesn't matter now if it's Paul or Amy.

I want to get out of here in one piece. I want to survive this, and the only way I'm going to get a chance to do that is if I get to the house before Amy gets to me.

I don't know how I know she's going to hurt me, but I do. I feel it in me as confidently as I know anything else. Amy is coming for me. I don't know if it's because she's just not happy I was having so much fun in Raleigh or if Paul got into her head.

I don't know if she's just upset with him and wants to take it out on me. There's no way for me to know what has gotten into her, but I saw my wife leave the cottage. I have no idea why she would choose Paul over me, why she would help him down to the cottage and take care of him before coming to hunt me, but that's exactly what she's doing.

Fear settles cold and hard in the pit of my stomach like a rock, and I groan, rubbing my free hand over my face. I feel weak, like every step I take is almost enough to bring me to my knees, but I have to keep going. Once I get in the house and lock myself in the kitchen, I'll be able to relax.

Even as I tell myself to move faster, though, I feel myself slowing down. My feet feel heavier and heavier, like someone has dipped them in concrete and it's set around them. My movements are clumsy, and it's getting harder for me to think straight.

How much blood have I lost?

I should call to my wife and try to talk this over with her. I think if the two of us could just sit down and talk things out, then she'd see I'm on her side. I'm not the one who was watching her through holes in the walls. I'm not the one who built some kind of sick shrine to her down in the basement.

The tip of my toe catches on a rock, and I pitch forward, landing hard on my knee. Moaning, I roll over onto my back, blinking up into the night sky. I hurried home to see my wife. I wanted to make sure she was safe and that she knew how much I loved her, but it's beginning to look like rushing home was pointless.

The soft crack of a twig snapping to my right makes me roll my head in that direction. I'm getting dizzy now, the edges of my vision blurry and dark. Maybe it's the night sky that looks so dark.

Maybe it's not. How much blood can you lose before you start to lose control of everything?

"Amy?" My tongue feels fat and thick in my mouth when I say my wife's name. "Amy."

She leans over me, blocking out the winking stars in the sky above.

I can't make out the expression on her face, but I still shiver away from her, wanting to put some distance between the two of us. There's nowhere to go, not with the cold, hard ground beneath me. Open sky stretches out behind her, but there's no way I can get her to move, no way I can get up.

"Not Amy," the woman says, and I swear I recognize her voice, but I can't quite place it.

41

PAUL

Holly left my cottage angry. Too angry. Her cheeks were the same hot red Wilma's used to get when she was upset about something and I wanted to stop her, but the searing pain in my side kept me from following Holly out the door.

I know Amy didn't mean to stab me. She wouldn't do that to me, wouldn't want to hurt someone like she did, especially not after she and I have gotten so close this week. Tim, on the other hand, would willingly hurt anyone just to get what he wanted, but not Amy. What happened between the two of us was an accident.

A misunderstanding. That's all it was. I'm sure of it. She was angry, that much was obvious, but I know she wasn't really angry at me. She was angry at Tim for being a terrible husband, for not being there for her. She'd never want to really hurt me, she just lashed out.

I knew all too well how people could do that. How many times, while I worked on a plan for revenge, had Holly lashed out at me? She was angry I was going too slow, that I was taking my time. She thought I should hurry up and get to the punch faster, just hurt Tim no matter what, but I knew we needed to wait for the perfect time. I moved to the cottage shortly after Wilma died and the bank took the house just to get out of the space I'd shared with my wife. Was it hard?

Of course it was.

But it's all working out now.

Holly hated waiting, but what she didn't realize is I know how to play the waiting game. I know how to make sure everything works out for me in the end, no matter how scary it might seem at first.

And it is. Sure, there's the minor setback of Amy not fully understanding I'm here for her and that everything I'm going to do is to help her, but she'll figure it out. I'll talk her down. I know her better than anyone else does. Tim may think he knows his wife, but I've watched her when she was alone, at her worst, and in need of help. I was there for her when nobody else was around to help her.

I know what to say to get her to calm down, to listen to reason.

But the only way I'm going to be able to fix all this and talk her down off the ledge she's perched on is to find her first. I have to make her see I was only taking care of her in the way she needed. I have to make her see I was willing to do what her husband wasn't.

She'll understand. She has to. The two of us have connected this week in a way I didn't think was entirely possible, but I hoped we would. She sees me for who I really am, and I can't imagine she would turn her back on me now, not when she needs someone on her side so badly.

What did Tim do as soon as things got rough? Ran. Like he does. But not me. I'm there for her. She'll see.

Groaning, I plant my hand on the table and push myself up. I'm wobbly, my legs weak, but I somehow force myself to put one foot in front of the other as I head towards the door. Each step brings me closer to finding Amy and stopping Holly from hurting her.

But I have to remember Tim is out there somewhere too. Groaning, I run the back of my hand across my forehead. Tim's the real problem here, the one we need to stop. He's the reason why Amy turned to me in the first place, why she couldn't be happy in her marriage. If he truly loved her and wanted to take care of her, then he wouldn't have left her to go to Raleigh.

And he certainly wouldn't have treated her the way he did. I saw her cry, heard her sobbing herself to sleep after we'd had dinner, and I know I'm the only person in the world who can help her right now.

Tim certainly isn't going to, and Holly's out to hurt her.

I can stop my daughter and calm her down. I'll make sure Amy is safe; then I'll be able to have both Holly and Amy in my life. Holly told me she was nice enough when they were buying the house, so I'm sure they'll get along. I just have to make sure they get that opportunity, and that means stopping Holly from hurting her.

I brace myself on the doorframe, my hand cramping from squeezing the wood so hard. Letting go is hard, but I have to force myself to relax my grip just so I can step outside. As soon as I do, I take a deep breath. Fresh air blows into my face, and I relax into it, trying to keep my feet under me.

Up the hill, past the garden I've been taking such good care of, and behind a crooked tree, I see the house. There are lights on inside, but nobody moves in front of the windows. If Amy has run up to the house to take refuge, then she's doing a really good job hiding.

But I don't think that's where she is. She was freaked out by the idea of me watching her when she was alone, but she doesn't get it. I have to explain it to her, make her see what I was really doing.

I swore to myself I would keep Amy safe, and now I have to do that. It kills me, sending a twisting pain through my heart, to think my daughter is so upset I might not be able to get her to see reason. That Holly is upset enough to take it all out on Amy.

I know that was the original plan, but plans change. Holly has to see that.

I lurch away from the cottage, swearing softly to myself as I put one foot in front of the other. It's so dark out here it's almost impossible to see where I'm going. If the clouds would just move away from the moon, then I might have an easier time knowing where to go to save Amy, but it's so dark out here all I can do is stumble forward, listening hard before each step.

I need a flashlight, but I don't have one with me. The garden, which is my favorite place to be during the day when I'm working in it and coaxing it into something beautiful that I love, is suddenly a battleground. I hesitate, my foot hovering above the ground before each step. I barely know my way around, not without some sort of lighting, not when there are so many people in my garden who want to hurt each other.

My heart beats so hard I feel heat radiating from my skin. I just ... I just don't know which way to go. The frustration of not knowing where Tim is hiding is driving me mad. My stab wound aches, each step sending a shooting pain through my body, and I know I really need a doctor, but it's not exactly like I can stop and call one.

No, I have to save Amy.

That means I have to kill Tim.

And Holly.

She's too far gone. I don't want it to be true, but at this point, I just want to keep Amy safe.

My fingers tighten at the realization, and the fact I don't have my clippers with me washes over me in horror. They're still in the cottage, and I turn back to get them. What I hear next makes the hairs on the back of my neck stand up and spurs me on.

42

AMY

I'm halfway to the cottage when my husband's screams from somewhere near the house stops me in my tracks. Fear rolls over me, making it difficult for me to breathe, and I drop to the cold ground, flattening myself as much as possible.

I should go to him, I know that, should try to protect him from Paul's attack, but I didn't realize he had left his cottage. Honestly, I thought he was still in there, licking his wounds, plotting his next move.

Tim's screams stop abruptly, like someone shut the door to a soundproof room. The night's oppressive silence resumes, feeling like a weighted blanket pressing me down.

"Tim?" I whisper, even though I know there's no way he'll hear me. There's no way he'll ever hear me again. I don't need to see his body to know things are over for him, but I still want to. A wave of nausea rolls over me when I think about never seeing him again. It feels like the connection between us has been broken, but I still want to see him.

I sink down into that thought, letting it wash over me. It's painful, sure, and I dig my fingers into the cold, hard ground as I try to come to grips with it.

Tim is gone.

Paul killed him.

Pushing myself up, I run towards the cottage, away from the house. It doesn't matter any longer if someone sees me moving around. They know I'm here. They're hunting us. Whoever Paul has with him in the gardens can't be a good person, they just can't. They must be as evil and creepy as he is.

Tim was closer to the house than I was, and now he's dead. I'm not going to the house. I'm hoping I can sneak into the cottage while nobody is looking.

I run down the hill to the cottage, my lungs screaming at me to slow down and take a deep breath. If Tim had listened to me and gotten us the landline like I'd wanted, then this wouldn't be happening. I wouldn't be running towards the cottage on the off chance that Paul will have a phone in there.

My cell phone is destroyed, and there's no way that I'm going to where Tim is. He's gone, and I don't want to meet whoever killed him.

I reach the cottage door but don't slow down, skidding right through it as I push it open, my heart pounding, my one hand gripping the knife as tightly as I can.

"Paul?" His name feels like acid on my tongue, like something evil I shouldn't ever say, and I stare at him. He's by the kitchen sink, his torso wrapped with bandages, his back bent. He's older than us, I knew that, but never has he looked this old before. "Paul, what the hell are you doing?"

This makes him turn, slowly, his hand reaching out to take his clippers from the counter. I'm wary, watching him with my body angled so I can see if anyone comes in through the door behind me.

"Amy, you're okay." There's a ton of relief in his voice, but I don't want to hear it.

"You killed Tim." It feels right to accuse him even though I don't know if I'm right. If Paul is here and in as rough shape as he looks, then I don't think he would have been able to kill my husband and beat me back here. That means the person who was with him, the person I saw running to the basement, *they* must have hurt Tim.

But I don't know if I believe it.

"I didn't. You have to believe me, Amy, this was all for you." He turns the rest of the way to me but doesn't put the clippers down.

"What was? Watching me? Spying on me?"

"I didn't mean to scare you. I wanted to protect you. Tim wasn't doing a good job of it. He left you."

"Tim," I say, then stop, my voice breaking on my husband's name. "Tim was doing what he had to for our family. He had to go to training. He had to—"

"He didn't have to make you think he was having an affair. He didn't have to make you cry. He didn't have to do those things, Amy."

Cool anger washes over me as I stare at him, but I don't speak. I'm honestly not sure what to say to him right now. Is he right? No. No, I can't believe that he is. "You don't know what you did," I say, but that's not right either. Paul knows what he did. He's staring at me with all the confidence in the world, like he honestly doesn't think he did anything wrong.

"I kept you safe. What if something had happened to you when you were here alone? It's a big house, with no security system, no landline. Cell phones are unreliable out here when it's stormy. What if you got hurt?" He takes a step closer to me, finally putting the clippers down behind him.

"You killed Tim," I say, lifting up my knife to stop him in his tracks. I stabbed him once. I'll do it again. I don't want to, don't want to relive the way the knife slipped into him like it was cutting through Jell-O and then raw meat. I don't want to remember the way he stared at me, his eyes slowly widening, until I pulled the knife free and ran.

Sticky blood coats the handle and my skin, and I feel like even if I tried to put the weapon down, I wouldn't be able to. It's stuck to me, a reminder of what I did.

"I didn't touch him," Paul tells me, gesturing to his side. "I've been in here, licking my wounds."

"But you know who did."

He nods.

"And you didn't stop them."

"I was going to stop them from hurting you. I wanted to keep you safe, not Tim. That's been the plan all along, Amy, to protect you. It's always been my goal. Tim doesn't do it, doesn't really care to try, but I was looking out for you. Always. You remind me so much of her, you know. Of Wilma."

"That wasn't the plan. Not always."

A woman's voice from behind me makes me spin around. I'm still holding the knife, and I swing it in the air between us as a warning for her to stay back.

"Seriously, Amy? After all we've been through?"

"Holly?" My hand wavers in the air, but I'm proud of myself for not lowering my weapon. I do shift position a little, just enough to keep the two of them in my sight. The cottage is too small for me to move as far away from them as I'd like to, but I inch away, just enough so I can see them both.

Holly sighs like she's disappointed it's taken me this long to figure it all out, but honestly I'm still in the dark. She's dressed in jeans and a hoodie, unlike the professional outfits I've seen her in before. When I manage to tear my eyes away from her face to take in the rest of her, I'm sickened when I see the crimson on the front of her clothes, the red on her hand.

It matches the blood on my hand, and my stomach sinks.

"You killed Tim." I hold my breath, not sure if I'm going to believe what she says.

She nods. "It was about time. You know, after he killed my mom, I wanted revenge right away, but Dad over here made me wait. He said the time wasn't right yet."

"Wait. Your dad?" I turn to Paul, my mind buzzing with this new information. I know what she said about Tim, but do I believe her? "Paul is your dad?"

Another nod, this one accompanied by a smile that's mostly teeth. "I reached out to you when you needed a great house. I helped you get it for a steal from the bank. I gave you my dad's name when you needed a caretaker. I did it all, Amy."

"Why? Just to hurt us?"

"To get back at you both for what you did to my mom. Tim killed her, you realize that, don't you?" She takes a step towards me.

I don't see a weapon in her hand, but I still step back, the feeling of the wall behind me causing my skin to crawl.

This cottage is too small. There's no way for me to get out of here, not with her standing in the doorway. Even if she were to move, I don't think I could make my legs respond. They feel like tree trunks, merged with the floor, and my fear is the roots keeping me here.

I was right about the cottage. Paul tricked me into thinking this place was a good place, a safe place. We had dinner down here, and I managed to lie to myself that it was safe, but I should have believed how I felt after the teacup incident. It's dangerous here, and I never should have come.

"Please," I say, and I hate myself for even letting the word pass my lips. I don't want to beg this woman, don't want to fall on her mercy to live. She's wild, her eyes wide and darting around the cottage like she's not sure what to do next, and fear settles hard and cold in my stomach. "Please, Holly. You don't want to do this."

"This?" Her laugh is mirthless. "This is exactly what I want to do."

"Holly, no." Paul's voice is weaker than I've heard it before. If his daughter hears him, she doesn't respond.

She's too busy coming for me.

43

AMY

I do the only thing I think will save me.

I run.

Right at Holly.

I should stab her, should try to keep her from ever coming for me again, but fear eats away at any rational thought I have, and I keep my knife clutched tightly in my hand instead of using it to save myself.

Paul can't protect me; he was too weak even standing there. I don't know if I hit anything vital when I stabbed him, but he was obviously struggling to stand. It would be insane for me to think he could help me.

Tim is gone. A sob grows in the back of my throat as I think about that, as I picture my husband out on the cold ground in the middle of the garden. Pushing that thought from my mind, I close the last few feet to the Realtor I trusted so badly and slam into her, knocking her off balance to the side. Holly stumbles, slamming into the doorframe as she cries out, but there's no way I'm going to slow down and listen to what she has to say.

The only thought running through my head right now is

that I need to get out of here. I have to run, have to try to get away from this woman who wants to kill me.

My lungs are on fire as I stumble-run my way up towards the house. I don't know what I'm going to do when I get there, maybe grab my car keys and make a run for it. If I can get in my car, then it won't matter that she's chasing me. I'll be halfway to freedom before she can catch up with me.

I just have to get to a car, get down the driveway, get into town. I know where the police station is, but I might be able to find a cop and get picked up just by speeding. I'll do something. Anything. The image of me leaning on my horn as I drive through town fills my head, and it's so real I actually think it's going to happen.

Then Holly slams into me from behind, throwing me to the ground. Searing pain shoots up through my wrists as I catch myself and roll over, lifting my arm to cover my face as she stands over me. The knife flies from my hand, and I grope out to the side for it, never taking my eyes off her face.

It's gone. I have no idea where it is, but there's no chance of me finding it in the dark now. My fingers close on a root, but that won't help me.

"You know, your husband didn't fight either," she tells me. There's a grin on her face that makes her look evil. Gone is the sweet Realtor I laughed with while we sent our offer letter to the bank. Gone is the woman I thought I could be friends with if she didn't work so much and had free time to get together.

"Don't do this," I beg her, scooting back from her. My palms are raw from the fall, but I barely notice the twinges of pain shooting through me as I move. "You don't have to do this, Holly. I wasn't involved. I didn't know. And Tim—"

"Please tell me you're going to throw your husband under the bus."

I shake my head. "He didn't know. You have to believe me,

Holly, he didn't know. He was horrified Marie would make him do something like that. He cried—" My voice breaks, and I stop talking.

"I bet I cried more at my mom's funeral." Her hand moves slowly to her side, and she pulls a knife from her pocket, flicking it hard so the blade swings out and locks into place.

The click is loud in the cool night air, and I tear my gaze from her hand to her face.

There's nothing there. No expression. The clouds have finally moved enough for some moonlight to reach us, but even in full daylight I don't think I'd be able to find any emotion written on this woman's face. She's too far gone, too wrapped up in her own anger.

"I have to do this," she tells me, like that's going to suddenly make me agree. When she raises her arms above her head, I wince, turning my head to the side so I don't have to watch what's about to happen.

"Move, Amy!" Paul's voice is loud and rips me out of my frozen state. When I look up, he's slamming into his daughter, knocking her off her feet and shoving her out of the way. "Go!"

He doesn't have to tell me twice. Scrabbling backwards to get some space between us, I finally stand and start running, my feet moving faster than I would have thought possible. I still feel like I'm having an out-of-body experience, like I'm going to wake up and realize this was a bad dream all along, but that doesn't slow me down.

I don't stop running until I'm in the house and grabbing my keys from the hook by the door. I need a weapon, something I can use to protect myself, but the thought of being in the house any longer than I have to is enough to make me feel sick. I could get another knife from the kitchen and bring it with me, or I could just run for it.

The screen door slams shut behind me as I tear back out

of the house to the driveway. Somewhere, in the garden, Paul and Holly are fighting, but I can't go down there. I can't help him, can't even think about turning away from my plan.

My fingers feel useless and numb when I try to find the right key. "Come on," I mutter, finally pressing down on the unlock button. The lights in my car blink once, then twice, and I rush to it, tears streaming down my face.

Then I stop.

My tires have been slashed. I drop to my knees, running my fingers over the rubber. "No, no, no," I mutter, panic gripping the back of my neck again. "No, this can't be happening."

Not just one, but all four. They've all been slashed, all of them useless. I fight back the bile in the back of my throat and turn back to the house, stumbling now, going slower than I was because I'm not sure what to do. My house isn't safe. Paul proved that to me, and there's no way I can hope Holly won't find her way in.

Stopping on the path to the front door, I listen hard, my mouth dry with fear. I don't hear anything, but that doesn't mean I'm safe. Just because I can't hear Holly coming for me doesn't mean she's not there.

Whispers in the back of my mind tell me to run, so I do, tearing up the front porch to the house. I'll barricade myself in a closet, something, anything. I'm grateful I didn't listen to Tim and lock the door earlier. Slamming it behind me, I throw the dead bolt, then rush to the kitchen.

And see Tim's jacket tossed on the table.

His phone is in the pocket.

"Oh, thank God," I say, grabbing it and typing in his passcode. My fingers fumble as I lift the phone to my ear, but then it finally rings, and I relax.

"911. What's your emergency?"

I freeze, looking down at my bloody hands. There's no way they're going to believe me when I tell them everything.

It's so far-fetched that I almost don't believe it myself. I have to wash up, have to find the knife I used to stab Paul.

I don't want to go to jail.

There's a rational part of me telling me I won't be arrested, that the police will understand everything, but I can't listen to that part of my brain right now.

"911. Is there an emergency?" The dispatcher sounds annoyed.

I swallow hard, trying to get my body to work the way I need it to. "He's going to kill me," I finally stammer. I don't think it's really true, not after what Paul was saying about loving me, not after he stopped Holly from hurting me, but it's the only thing running through my mind.

Watching me from between the walls. Taking my things to build a shrine. Stabbing Tim.

"Who is going to kill you? Are you in a safe location right now? I need your address." Gone is whatever disinterest the dispatcher had a moment ago when she probably thought I was just prank calling her. She's all professionalism now, and I hear her typing what I just said.

Relief floods through me, but then I seize in fear. Am I safe right now?

Turning around, I eyeball the walls. He could be anywhere. He could be watching and listening to me right now, laughing to himself about me calling for help when he's still so close. The tiny hairs on the back of my neck stick straight up, and I shiver, backing up until I'm pressing against the counter.

I rattle off my address without really stopping to think about it, but now I have to give her the rest of the information she wants, and I hesitate. *Am I safe?* "I don't know," I whisper, my eyes darting from side to side. "I don't know if I'm safe."

"Okay, ma'am, I need you to try to get somewhere safe. Is there anyone else there with you who can help you?

Anywhere you can go where you're going to be protected?" She's all business.

"No," I whisper, shaking my head. "There isn't anywhere. You don't understand, he's ... he's everywhere. He's in the house; he's in the walls ..." I know I sound like a crazy person, but I need her to understand what's going on. "You have to hurry! They killed my husband, and now he's—"

A scream cuts off my words. *Holly.*

"Oh, God, he killed Holly," I whisper, my finger suddenly going clammy. "He killed his own daughter, don't you see? Please, you have to help me! You have to hurry!"

"I have officers already dispatched to your location. I need you to stay on the phone with me, okay? Please do not hang up the phone."

I know I should do what she's asking me to do, but I can't. I can't just sit here in the kitchen and wait for him to come for me. I have no way of knowing if he's going to waltz right in through the front door like he owns the place or if he's going to come through the walls.

A whimper escapes my lips, and my eyes dart back and forth from the front door to where he hung the picture on the wall to block his peephole. *He knew it was there.* He knew it was there, and he still pretended like he had no idea what I was talking about.

And what's worse is I believed him. I made him dinner and laughed with him. I spilled my guts to him about my problems with Tim, but instead of just being supportive, he was planning to kill my husband all along.

"I can't be in here," I whisper to the dispatcher. I know she's going to argue with me and tell me it's safer for me to stay on the phone with her, but she's wrong.

There isn't anything *safer* here. Not with Paul around. Not when he could easily sneak up on me and I'd never know.

I think something is behind me, and I whip around, my

legs feeling weak. I can't keep my eyes on all the places where he might pop up. I can't be in the house.

"I have to run," I tell her, then hang up, cutting off her complaints. It's stupid, and I'm sure of it, but I can't hide outside talking on the phone when I need to be as quiet as possible. I can't have her voice carrying through the night air, not when Paul is looking for me.

Because he is.

I know it.

44

AMY

The junk drawer clatters loudly when I pull it out and reach in, digging around for the brightest flashlight we have. It feels good in my hand, weighty, with a strong beam, but it's not in here, and I shove the drawer closed again before turning for the front door.

Once I step out there, I'll know for sure what happened to Tim. I'll know if Holly survived. I'll know it all. My eyes fall on the smaller flashlight on the kitchen counter, and I grab it, pressing the button to turn it on before sweeping it slowly around the room. It gives off a weak beam that falters a little, but it's still the best option I have.

Leaving the house, I move quickly down to the cottage, no longer worried about being quiet. There's a soft glow coming from across the garden. It has to be the lights inside the cottage, and I use it to orient myself so I don't shoot past my destination.

I have no idea what I'm going to do, but I do know I have to hide. I want to see Tim, even though Holly said she killed him, and I run down the path through the garden towards the koi pond.

I don't know exactly where I'm going, but I do know I need to keep moving. I need to find Tim. I need to hide from Paul. I think he killed Holly—*killed his own daughter*—which means he's more terrifying than I ever thought before.

But as I turn towards the cottage, everything changes.

"What the hell?" The soft glow I thought to be the cottage lights has exploded upward, changing from the welcoming light of the cottage to the fierce blaze of a fire. I stumble forward, driven on not only by fear but the knowledge I have to get down there as soon as possible if I'm going to figure anything out.

"Tim!" I scream for my husband even though I know he's dead. It's silly to call for him, but I can't help his name escaping from my lips. "Tim!"

Nothing. Of course, nothing. It's not like I can suddenly turn back time and bring him back, but a shiver still runs up my spine as I hurry towards the cottage. My foot kicks something, sends it spinning, and I reach to the ground to pick up the knife I used to stab Paul.

Fear grips the back of my neck. I need to get to the cottage, need to know why the hell Paul started the blaze, but I spin to the side and run to the koi pond, where I drop the bloody knife. I'm panicking and I know that. I don't want anyone to tie me to stabbing Paul. Tears spring to the corners of my eyes when I think about the look on his face when I stabbed him. But I had to.

He hurt Tim. I didn't know if he was going to hurt him again.

I didn't know if he was going to hurt me.

And now I have to hide. This was stupid, hanging up on the dispatcher and running outside because I thought I would find Tim or could hide from Paul. Now I realize just how exposed I am out here, how very dangerous it is for me to be out in the open without any sort of protection.

Part of me regrets dropping the knife into the pond, but at the same time I know there's no way I could stab Paul again. My stomach turns when I think about how easily the knife slid into his side, how his eyes widened and his mouth formed a surprised little O when I hurt him.

I just have to run.

Spinning around, I turn my back on the burning cottage. There's a little voice in the back of my mind screaming at me to keep moving, and I drop the flashlight, useless thing, and dig my shoes into the dirt to take off towards the house.

"Amy." Paul's voice makes my head snap up.

He's right in front of me, hunched over slightly like it would hurt too much for him to straighten up. His shirt is blood-soaked, and I have to tear my eyes away from the dull crimson to look up at his face, which is twisted in pain. Still, even though it's obvious he's badly hurt, he stares at me, his eyes filled with kindness.

"Paul, I need you to let me go." I say the words as calmly as possible. I don't know how he's going to react. I have no idea if he'll hurt me because I stabbed him. I have no idea where Tim and Holly are, and I'm certain I should never have left the house.

But he just shakes his head.

"You stabbed me," he says, his voice surprisingly calm. "You tried to kill me when I was just taking care of you."

"Taking care of me?" My voice pitches too high. "You stabbed Tim! You tried to kill my husband!"

"To save you! I love you!" He grits the words out at me, taking a step towards me.

I move backwards, not wanting him anywhere near me.

"I did it all to save you, do you not get that? Everything I did was to keep you safe! I love you, Wilma."

"Wilma?" I can't believe what I just heard him say, but if he realizes he's called me by his dead wife's name, he doesn't show it. His eyes are still locked on me like he's never been happier to see a person in his life.

"Amy." He corrects himself, shaking his head a little, but doesn't give me an explanation. "Amy, I love you. I did all this to keep you safe, to make sure you would have the life you deserve. Tim didn't deserve you. He broke your heart, but I won't ever do that."

"You two killed him. You," I say, pointing at him, "did this." I wish I hadn't thrown the knife away. What if he tries to hurt me now? What if he won't let me go and I can't protect myself?

"No. I didn't. Holly did, Amy, and she was going to kill you too. I killed her to save you. I protected you, Amy, even though that meant I had to say goodbye to my little girl."

I remember how he knocked her out of the way when she was on top of me. I remember her scream cutting through the night.

"Where is he? His ..." I can't finish the question, can't ask where Tim's body is. "Where's Tim? I want to see him." I shake my head, trying to clear it. Maybe he's not dead. Maybe Holly was lying, trying to upset me. Maybe Paul has been lying. Tim could be alive, injured but alive, and the longer I stand here talking to Paul, the more likely it is he won't make it.

"Don't you see I freed you?" Ignoring my question, Paul steps closer to me.

I move back again, keeping the distance between us.

"Why would you want to go to him now when you're finally free?"

"I love him," I manage. The words leave my mouth in painful gasps, and I feel like I'm choking. "I love him! You took him from me!"

"He didn't deserve you!" This is the first time I've seen Paul angry. His eyes are dark, and he stares at me like he honestly can't believe I don't get it. "He didn't deserve you, Amy, but I love you. I did this so we can be together."

"What?" I whisper, taking another step back from him. The koi pond is right behind me, and I need to be careful, but I don't think I can handle being this close to him. The air feels tight, like it's difficult for me to breathe, and I need to put some space between the two of us. "You've lost it, Paul."

He doesn't respond.

Over the sound of the roaring fire, I hear sirens. We're running out of time, but I still don't know what to do. The police are coming, they're close enough for me to realize I'm almost safe from this nightmare, but I still don't know what to do about Paul.

"Come with me." He reaches his hand out towards me, his eyes bright with excitement. "Amy, come with me, and I promise you, nobody will ever hurt you again. I promise you I'll take care of you. I'll keep you happy, keep you safe. You're everything, you know that, right? You remind me so much of her."

"Of Wilma."

He nods, then grimaces, pressing down harder on his side.

It's probably really bad for him to be on his feet and talking like this. He probably should have been in surgery already to survive. He's losing a lot of blood, and I don't know how much longer he'll last.

"Please, Amy," he whispers.

I just shake my head and take another step back from him.

His hand wavers in the air between us for a moment before he drops it, flashes of regret and anger mixing across his face as he stares at me. "You'll see how much I love you," he promises me. "I won't leave you."

His words send a horrible chill up my spine that snakes

through my body, freezing me from the inside. I stare back at him in shock. "Paul, I don't love you," I say. "I hope you rot in jail for all you've done to me and Tim. I hope I never see you again." My words drip with anger, but I need them to. I need him to know what he's done to me.

"You'll see," he tells me, finally taking a step back. "You'll see that you belong with me. I lost my Wilma and thought I'd never survive it, but then I met you, and I knew I would. You're here to be mine, Amy. You're here to take her place, to let me remember her by loving you."

"You're insane!" I scream, hoping the cops will hear me and come running. They have to be here by now, right? Ash falls around us like black snow, resting so lightly on my skin that I don't feel it. My eyes are locked on Paul's face.

"I'll tell them," I say. "The police. I'll tell them you killed them. I'll tell them everything, about the stuff you stole, how you moved around in the walls, about you watching me!" My mind flashes back to the little setup he had of my things, how everything was placed just perfectly so it looked its best. I remember how he scratched out Tim's face, how the scent of my perfume had filled the air. "You'll rot in jail, Paul."

"I was taking care of you." He takes a step towards me again, reaching out his hand like he wants me to meet him halfway.

I don't.

I can't.

He was watching me while I slept. Shivers crawl up my body, and I shake my head. "I never want to see you again."

"Amy, I love you."

"You love me?" Cold dances up my spine, and I stare at him in horror. I want him to leave. I never want to see this man again. There's nothing I'd love more than for him to rot in jail for the rest of his life. Tears spring to my eyes and burn there, but I don't let them fall.

"Amy, I—" he begins.

But I cut him off. "You don't love me. You tortured me! You're the reason Tim is dead! That's not love, that's insanity!" I scream, willing him to disappear. I need him to go so that I can breathe again. Right now, even though we're outside, the air feels tight and heavy, like I can't take a deep enough breath to really fill my lungs. "I never want to see you again! I hate you!"

He looks like I've slapped him and finally takes a faltering step back from me, his eyes wide. "I love you," he repeats, his voice so sad that, for a moment, I almost feel bad for him.

"You're a monster. I hope you rot in jail for the rest of your life." Turning from him, I look up at the driveway. The sound of sirens is growing closer. If they hurry, they can make it in time to catch him. If they hurry, they can take him to jail, lock him up. He'll never be able to hurt people again.

But when I look back, Paul's gone.

He's like a ghost, there one moment and gone the next, and I'm left blinking by the koi pond as flashing red and blue lights rip across the sky.

"Here!" I jump up and down, waving my arms in the air to get their attention.

Two police cars screech to a halt by my car in the driveway, then the doors open, and the officers make their way through the garden to me.

"I'm down here!" I call, then wrap my arms around myself and shiver.

My mind races as they approach. I see one pause and turn back towards the cottage, bending his neck to his shoulder like he's speaking into his radio. Probably calling for a fire truck, I realize, but it's going to be too late by the time they get here. There's absolutely no saving the cottage, Paul made sure of it.

"Are you okay?" The officer reaches me, her face pale, her eyes flicking from left to right as she takes in the scene.

I realize immediately how I must look, and even though I'm trying to stay strong, my knees give way, and I sink to the ground in relief. "He's gone," I tell her. "I'm okay, but my husband, he's dead." My mind races. "Oh, God, he's dead. The fire ..."

"Is anyone inside?" She was resting her hand on her gun but now has her hand on her radio, ready to call for more help, and she squats next to me. "The cottage. Is anyone inside?"

I swallow hard. "No, but he's—" Turning, I gesture towards the woods. They're so deep and dark there's no seeing into them now. Paul's in there somewhere, and while I can't see him, I know one thing.

He's still watching.

45

AMY

It's been two months since I stood, wrapped in a scratchy gray blanket an EMT had wrapped around my shoulders, and watched as the cottage burned to ashes.

I showed the police everything. The remains of the shrine to me, how Paul was able to move through the double walls of the house. They took pictures, took my statement, and gave me a hot cup of coffee I couldn't make myself drink.

It felt really good to hold it in my hands though, and I did that, squeezing the flimsy sides as I gripped it like it was the one thing that could take this nightmare away. But it didn't, and when the coffee was finally as cold as the night air, I poured it on the dry ground, watching in the dim light of the rising sun as it soaked into the dirt.

I know some people in town thought I killed my husband for sure, but there was no proof.

The police said I was innocent, and that was that. There was no proof I murdered Holly or Tim, no proof I did anything wrong. I was just unlucky enough to catch the eye of a creepy man who didn't know how to take no for an answer.

My hands shake as I open up a newspaper and spread it out in front of me. My therapist told me I can't stay locked up in my apartment forever and that I need to get out and make sure I'm living my life as much as possible, but it's really hard. This is my first trip out for a cup of coffee since that horrible cup the night everything changed.

It sits next to me, a gingerbread latte. I'm sure it would be delicious if I could just make myself drink it, but I can't seem to force myself to take a sip. Instead, I spread my hands out over the paper, smoothing it so I can read it.

I'm looking for any article that mentions what happened at the house. It's for sale, with a Realtor I've never met, and I hope to never see the house again. All I want is to end that chapter of my life, move on, and pretend like it never happened.

That's why I moved to a new town about an hour away. Nobody here knows who I am; nobody knows what I went through back home. I saw one mention of the two murders in this paper soon after I moved, but nothing since then.

Nothing. I'm safe. I haven't seen hide nor hair of Paul, but I'm fully prepared to call the police if he ever shows up again. I have a state-of-the-art security system at home that makes me feel safe when I'm asleep, although I don't get more than a few hours a night. I still think I feel someone watching me, but it's impossible.

He's not here. This is a new building with paper-thin walls, not an old mansion with double walls wide enough for someone to walk around in. I know there's no way he could find me here. He's probably dead from the stab wound I inflicted. Chances are really good he bled out in the woods behind the house, and they just never found his body.

That's a thing, right?

Shaking that thought from my head, I fold up the paper and push it to the side before picking up my latte and leaving the coffee shop. It's bright in there, almost too bright for my liking, and I'm ready to go back home. Jenna, my therapist, will be thrilled I left my apartment and went to a public place, but I feel like I need to get back home to recharge my batteries.

It's a quick two-block walk to my new apartment building. When I was looking for someplace to live, I told the rental company I wanted to be up high so nobody could look into my windows, and that I wanted to be close enough to the police station in case there was a problem. They're a few miles away, but all the closer apartment buildings were full, so this is the best I could do.

Hurrying up the flights of stairs, I unlock my door and step inside quickly before turning to lock the door and throw the safety bar at the top. Then I slide the chain along the top of the door into place.

All my doors and window have extra security systems on them just so I can sleep at night. Reaching up, I press my finger against the alarm pad to set the alarm, and then relax, leaning my forehead against the door for a moment. It's cool and sturdy, and I exhale hard, sagging against it in relief.

I never see my landlord, but that's okay. We've never met in person since I let the rental company handle everything for me. After signing the contract online, the key was delivered to the hotel I was staying at, and I moved out.

My landlord hadn't cared that I asked him to replace my door with one without a mail slot and with a peephole, especially when I offered to foot the bill. All that mattered to him was that I was quiet, neat, and paid my rent on time.

Not a problem.

Lifting the slats of the blinds, I look outside, my eyes scanning from right to left as I take in the sidewalk below me. It's not that I actually expect someone to be out there looking up at me, but it's habit.

I like to make sure nobody glances up here. They have no reason to. Out of all the buildings in the city, this is just one more, just a brown apartment building a little ways from downtown. I can walk to the store, although I prefer to have my groceries delivered. My copywriting clients don't care that I prefer not to leave my house.

They don't know I look out this window every fifteen minutes, or that I make the delivery people drop the groceries outside my door and leave before I open it.

My therapist keeps telling me it's time for me to come in and meet her face-to-face, but the reason I hired her was because she was willing to work with me over Zoom. I don't want to meet her, don't want to leave my apartment. I want to be here, in my small apartment, where I know nobody can get me.

Walking to the kitchen, I check the windows here, then head back to my desk. It's in the spare bedroom I've set up to operate as my office. After flicking on the light, I walk to the window, leaning forward to look through the blinds. Not a lot of people walk around the back of the apartment building. They're much more used to walking around the front.

But still, you can never be too certain.

I feel my shoulders relax when I see there isn't anyone out there. I'm fine; I'm safe. I don't need to worry about someone trying to hurt me. My therapist keeps telling me trauma will rule my life only if I let it, but it's really hard not to let it take control.

After I moved, I just knew I had to hide. I didn't want Paul to find me. It was just all the things he said about wanting to make sure I was safe and wanting to protect me because he loved me ... how do you know if you've left your past in the past?

I've already dumped my latte, but something in this room

smells really good. It's deep and musky, the scent filling the air, and I sniff it, lifting my nose to try to figure out what it is.

It's familiar, but I can't put my finger on it. I've smelled it before plenty of times, but the scent feels like more of a memory than anything tangible I can reach out and grab. Turning, I look around for a candle I may have left burning, but I already know there won't be one. I'm careful about that, to the point where I've come back into the room three or four times just to make sure I put the candle out.

So what is it?

It hits me.

It's the perfume I used to wear, the same scent Paul stole from my bedroom. I haven't worn it since smelling it in the basement. Right now it feels like it's choking me, and I back towards the door, my eyes wide as I look around the room.

Is he here?

It's impossible he could be in here. Impossible he would be able to make it up to my apartment and past the security system without me knowing about it. Impossible he could spray the perfume in here for me to smell later, but there's no mistaking the scent in the air, no mistaking the taste of bile at the back of my throat when I realized what it was.

Then I look across the room at the small table set up against the wall. That's where I keep a candle, well away from the wall and any paper so nothing will accidentally catch on fire. It's not burning, but it's moved closer to the picture frame I placed by it.

"No," I whisper, reaching up and grabbing at my throat like I can stop the word escaping my lips. "No, it's not possible."

It's the same ornate frame from the house. I'd had another photo printed for the frame. The police took the picture with Tim's eyes scratched out as evidence, and I never got it back.

Tim gave me the frame, and the only reason I kept it was because of him. I hated it, always have, but I brought it with me when I came here instead of getting rid of it.

I just couldn't. But now I wish I had.

"No, no, no," I say, still whispering like staying quiet is going to stop something terrible happening. Grabbing the picture, I look closer, not wanting to believe what I'm seeing.

It's a picture of Tim and me when we were dating, just before we got engaged. We look so young, so happy. You can see the huge grins on our faces and how mine reaches my eyes.

But not Tim's eyes.

Because his are all scratched out.

THANK YOU FOR READING

Did you enjoy reading *The Caretaker*? Please consider leaving a review on Amazon. Your review will help other readers to discover the novel.

ABOUT THE AUTHOR

Emily Shiner always dreamed of becoming an author but first served her time as a banker and a teacher. After a lifetime of devouring stacks of thrillers, she decided to try her hand at writing them herself. Now she gets to live out her dream of writing novels and sharing her stories with people around the world. She lives in the Appalachian Mountains and loves hiking with her husband, daughter, and their two dogs.

ALSO BY EMILY SHINER

Printed in Great Britain
by Amazon